I0774977

Something Wicked This Way Hums

Music Shop Mysteries, Book 2

Jennifer Lamont Leo

Mountain Majesty Media

SOMETHING WICKED THIS WAY HUMS

Published by Mountain Majesty Media, Inc.

PO Box 638, Cocolalla, Idaho 83813

ISBN 979-8-9901647-6-5 (e-book)

ISBN 979-8-9901647-7-2 (print)

ISBN 979-8-9901647-8-9 (audio)

Copyright © 2025 by Jennifer Lamont Leo

Cover design by Dee Dee Book Covers

For information on this book or author, visit www.jenniferlamontleo.com

All rights reserved.

No part of this publication may be reproduced, distributed, or transmitted in any form or by any means, including photocopying, recording, or other electronic or mechanical methods, without the prior written permission of the publisher, except as permitted by U.S. copyright law.

The story, all names, characters, and incidents portrayed in this production are fictitious. No identification with actual persons (living or deceased), places, buildings, and products is intended or should be inferred.

Printed in the United States of America

Chapter One

Timber Coulee, Idaho. May 1918.

"Amanda Parrish, don't you dare tell me you're too busy." Heidi Fischer planted herself in front of my sales counter, her determined expression at odds with her normally cheerful demeanor. "The Meadowlarks need you."

To avoid my friend's pleading blue eyes, I concentrated on unpacking a new shipment of sheet music that had just arrived at my humble emporium, the Mountain Melodies Music Shop. The early May breeze floated in around the two grunting workmen who were carefully maneuvering an upright piano through the shop door—the Whitakers' donation to replace the one damaged in last winter's leaky-pipe incident.

No sooner had they cleared the doorway than a well-dressed woman entered, glancing around with quiet appreciation at the rows of gleaming instruments. Around my age—mid-thirties—she wore a dove-gray walking suit, with her dark hair pinned neatly beneath a matching hat. I'd seen her around town once or twice, from a distance, but hadn't yet made her acquaintance.

"Welcome to Mountain Melodies," I called. "I'll be with you in a moment."

She tossed a smile in my direction before making her way to the classical piano music section.

Turning back to Heidi, I tried to let her down gently. "My schedule is busy enough already without adding the ladies' choir to the mix. Besides, I already let the Meadowlarks meet in my back storage room for rehearsals, free of charge. Isn't that enough?"

Heidi doubled down on her plea. "That *was* enough, until the Swanson girls left for France. Now we're desperate for altos." She picked up my orange tabby cat, who'd been methodically unknotting a ball of grayish-green yarn that had tumbled from her bag. "Even Moxie agrees—don't you, sweet boy?"

He purred and head-butted her chin. Traitor.

Heidi's honest admission that she was begging out of desperation, and not out of any particular admiration for my singing voice, did not increase my eagerness to help.

"Hurray for the Swanson girls," I said. "The Red Cross has greater need of nurses than your choir has of altos."

"The Red Cross isn't preparing to sing at the mayor's patriotic fundraiser on Memorial Day," she retorted.

The dark-haired woman approached the counter with a book of Chopin nocturnes. "Excuse me. Do y'all happen to have any Debussy?" Her voice carried the smooth, unhurried cadence of the Deep South, yet her correct pronunciation of "Debussy" impressed me. Most folks didn't get it right. "I didn't see it with the other composers," she added.

"We do." Grateful for the interruption, I swept my arm toward a smaller display by the window. "We just received a new shipment this week. There's been a small surge in demand since the composer's recent demise."

"Wonderful." She smiled, revealing a small dimple in her right cheek. "I'm Eleanor Crawford, by the way. I've admired your shop from afar but never had the pleasure of comin' in before."

"Amanda Parrish." I extended my hand. "And this is Heidi Fischer."

"Pleasure to meet you both." Eleanor's grip was gentle yet firm. "I've seen y'all around town, of course. Timber Coulee is charmingly small that way."

"Are you new to the area?" Heidi inquired, ever the social butterfly.

"Relatively speakin'. I've been here about six weeks now. I'm the new Western states correspondent for *Angel of the Hearth* magazine—have y'all heard of it?—and I'm writin' a series of articles on how small-town women are supportin' the war effort." She nodded toward the "Buy Bonds" poster in my window. "Your community has been wonderfully welcomin'."

"Well, we're glad to have you," I said. "Let me know if you need help finding anything else."

"Thank y'all." She turned toward the Debussy display with a graceful little nod.

Heidi immediately reclaimed my attention. "So? The choir? Please say yes."

She meant well. The community choir meant the world to her. The Rocky Mountain Meadowlarks Ladies' Choral and Knitting Society, to be exact. The "knitting" bit had been tacked on a few months earlier when word came down that our brave fighting men were in desperate need of warm socks. Now every rehearsal combined singing with knitting. But as a former choir member, I could think of a dozen things I'd rather be doing with my spare time. There were good reasons my membership was former, and one of them was just now walking through the door.

Mary Alice Wellington swept in, followed by two of her cronies. With only the briefest glance toward Heidi and me, they picked their way past the neat rows of instruments, forming expressions of mild distaste as they passed the sweaty-faced workmen.

"'Evening, ladies," I said. Mary Alice responded with a curt nod as they hustled to the back room.

"Come on," Heidi wheedled. "Even Molly's joined us. It'd be a fun activity you two could do together."

"We're not joined at the hip, you know."

Why did she have to bring my niece into the conversation? I loved Molly as if she were my own daughter, and we got along well. But after working together in the shop all day, it was nice to have the house to myself on the nights she went to choir practice, or out with friends or with her beau, Clarence Butterworth—before he'd gone off to war, of course.

From the corner of my eye, I saw Eleanor Crawford moving deeper into the shop, examining the instruments with quiet interest. She paused by a violin display, running one gloved finger lightly along the polished wood. A fellow classical music lover, perhaps? I made a mental note to tell her about our town's summer music camp in case, as a newcomer, she might not know about it.

"Come on, Amanda. Say yes." Like a dog with a bone, Heidi would not drop the subject. My resolve wavered in the face of her earnest plea. It began to feel like a patriotic duty to fill in for the brave Swanson girls, off to serve their country in a far-off land under dangerous circumstances. Like Clarence, and the Fairmont boy, and so many others. The sacrifice of joining the choir seemed minuscule by comparison. I tried not to think about the quiet evening I'd planned—a cup of tea, my current mystery novel, and absolutely no one demanding anything of me.

Choir members continued to enter the shop and head toward the back room. Heidi set Moxie down, retrieved the ball of yarn, tucked it into her bag, and started to say something. At the back of the shop, the workmen settled the piano to the floor with a bang.

"Careful, gentlemen," I warned.

"Sorry, lady." The men rolled the piano into the back room amid the *oohs* and *aahs* of the singers.

Heidi ignored the commotion. Her tone softened. "It would be like the old days. You used to love singing in the choir, especially alongside Sarah Holcomb. Remember what fun the two of you had? Always giggling over something or other, and causing trouble like a couple of schoolgirls. She'd want nothing more than for you—"

"Don't." The word came out sharper than I intended. We both knew our friend Sarah would have already coaxed me into joining, probably with that gentle persistence she'd perfected as the sheriff's wife. But Sarah wasn't here. She'd never be here again. After three years, the reality of her death still stung.

Heidi reached across the counter and covered my hand with hers. "I'm sorry. I shouldn't have. It's just, we really do need you, Amanda. And maybe it would be good for you to—"

"Fine." I withdrew my hand from hers and lifted the pile of sheet music. "But only until the Swanson girls return."

"Which will be soon. They say the war will be over by Christmas."

"I don't have a whole lot of confidence in what *they* say," I grumbled. "*They* promised to keep us out of the war in the first place. 'He kept us out of war,' indeed."

"But you'll do it?"

Her persistence wore me down. "Yes. Against my better judgment."

I straightened the sheet music with perhaps more force than necessary. My Bible reading that morning from Ecclesiastes had said "to everything there is a season." I supposed this was the season for me to return to the choir—whether I liked it or not.

Heidi's triumphant smile suggested she'd planned this ambush carefully. "Rehearsal starts in five minutes. I'll help you close up shop."

Eleanor approached with several sheets of music and placed them on the counter. "Just these, please." Each syllable stretched like taffy in the summer heat. "The Debussy is exactly what I was lookin' for."

As I tallied the purchases, she dabbed her nose with a handkerchief, and her eyes were red. Had she been crying?

Concerned, but not wanting to pry, I peered at her. "Everything all right?"

She fluttered the handkerchief. "Oh, don't mind me, sugar. It's just all this pollen floatin' around."

I grimaced in sympathy. "Others are suffering, too. Talk to Mr. Bates down at the drugstore. He's certain to have something to help you."

"Thank y'all." She jerked her head toward the stockroom. "Did I overhear that there's a choir rehearsin' back there?"

"The Meadowlarks," Heidi confirmed proudly. "We're preparing for the Memorial Day fundraiser for Liberty Bonds at the town hall. Do you sing, Miss Crawford? We're always looking for new members."

"It's Mrs. And just piano, I'm afraid." The dimple in her cheek deepened. "Although I've done a fair amount of accompanyin' vocalists."

"We do have a regular accompanist," Heidi said, "but it might be good to have another in reserve."

"I'll keep it in mind." Eleanor accepted her wrapped purchases. "Although I'm not certain how long the magazine will be keepin' me in town. Could be weeks or months. Well, thank you, Miss Parrish. I'll make a point of returnin' soon."

"You're welcome anytime," I replied.

She turned to leave, then paused to admire a display of harmonicas near the door. Equally eager to both make an additional sale and close up shop, I hovered near the cash register.

"I'll save you a seat next to me." Heidi headed toward the back room.

"All done, lady." I'd forgotten all about the piano movers. I settled business with the workmen, and by the time they left, Eleanor had vanished. I let in a few straggling choristers, then locked the door and flipped the window sign to Closed.

"Amanda, come *on*," Heidi called from the curtained doorway that separated the storage-room-turned-rehearsal-space from the rest of the shop. As I trudged to join her, I couldn't shake the feeling I'd just been neatly maneuvered into doing something I'd regret.

Chapter Two

As the director, Judith Hensley, called the rehearsal to order, Heidi gestured for me to sit next to her in the alto section.

"Welcome, Amanda." Judith beamed in my direction. "Heidi said you'd be joining us."

"Did she?" I shot my friend a look.

She responded with a sheepish grin and a shrug.

"And we also must take a moment to thank Honey Whitaker for the donation of the piano, after our old one suffered water damage," Judith continued. Murmurs of appreciation rippled through the group. With a gracious nod, Honey acknowledged their thanks.

Judith rapped a baton on her music stand. "All right, ladies. We have less than a month to prepare for the patriotic fundraiser called for by our mayor. And we still have much work to do. To that end, we will temporarily increase our practices from Mondays only to twice a week, Mondays and Thursdays."

Mary Alice raised her hand. "Thursdays won't work for some of us. That's when the Ladies' Aid meets. We're doing important war work, you know." Her tone implied that no one else in town could be bothered to lift a finger.

Judith pinched the bridge of her nose as if she were developing a headache, as I most certainly was. "All right. Those of you in Ladies' Aid are excused from the Thursday practices. But I trust the rest of you will make every effort to be here. As I said, these extra rehearsals are only temporary, just to get us through the fundraiser. We want this to be our best performance ever on behalf of our boys overseas, don't we?" General nods and murmurs of agreement dotted the room. Judith rapped her baton again. "Now, let's start with 'Battle Hymn of the Republic,' from the top. Mary Alice, will you take the solo in the third verse?"

"Again?" Beatrice Fairmont's voice cut through the rustling of music pages with the sharpness of a razor. "Mary Alice is already leading on 'The Star-Spangled Banner' and 'God Bless America.' I thought we'd agreed to rotate the solos, Judith." Her knuckles whitened around her knitting needles.

Mary Alice's posture stiffened. "We agreed to assign solos based on ability, Beatrice. Not everyone can reach the high notes with the proper . . . quality." She emphasized the last word with a saccharine smile. "Some voices simply have more patriotic fervor than others."

"Patriotic fervor?" Beatrice's knitting needles stilled as she stared at Mary Alice with undisguised hostility. "My quality was good enough for the carol-sing last Christmas. The newspaper called my rendition 'soaring and stirring,' if you recall."

"Was that before or after your cousin became editor of the *Timber Coulee Gazette*?" Mary Alice asked sweetly.

Several choir members gasped, and beside me, Heidi winced.

Judith rapped her baton again. "Ladies, please. We've discussed this repeatedly. Mary Alice's soprano range extends to high C, which is technically better suited for the Battle Hymn's challenging descant."

"My range is perfectly adequate," Beatrice insisted, her face flushing an alarming shade of crimson. "I've been taking extra lessons with Professor Wilson in Coeur d'Alene, and he says my upper register has improved tremendously."

"Perhaps in another year, then," Mary Alice said with false sympathy. "When you've had more time to . . . develop."

Beatrice's eyes narrowed to dangerous slits. "You think you're untouchable because you're treasurer of the Ladies' Aid, but some of us know things about you that would—"

"Enough!" Judith's baton cracked against her music stand, causing everyone to jump. "Beatrice, you'll take the solo in 'America the Beautiful.' Mary Alice, the 'Battle Hymn.' This is final."

"Second prize, as usual," Beatrice muttered just loud enough for the entire room to hear. "That one's not even a full stanza long." She jabbed her knitting needles into her yarn with such force that I half expected them to snap.

"Such a relief to be performing some good *American* music," Mary Alice remarked as she found her place, "after all those *German* songs at Christmas."

"Oh, please. 'Silent Night' isn't just a German song anymore," Beatrice countered. "It belongs to everybody now."

"Ladies, focus, *please*." With her smile still frozen in place, Judith nodded to Mildred Abernathy at the piano. The introduction began, and for a few blessed minutes, music overrode the tension. I glanced around the room as we sang and noticed a dark-haired girl of about sixteen, sitting in the soprano section next to Molly, who wasn't singing with the same enthusiasm as the others. While others sat straight-backed with chins lifted, her shoulders curved inward slightly. She looked vaguely familiar, but I couldn't place her.

The clicking of knitting needles kept perfect time with the music until Mary Alice lurched to her feet with a loud cry and slapped her music folder closed. Judith nearly dropped her baton. With a discordant crash, Mildred Abernathy brought the piano accompaniment to a halt and swiveled around on the bench to see what was going on.

"I simply cannot sing under these conditions!" Mary Alice cried. I half expected her to fall into a swoon, like a heroine in a Victorian melodrama. Instead, she glared at the startled faces of the choir.

"How am I supposed to concentrate with that infernal clicking?" she thundered.

I caught Molly's eye as she paused in her own sock-knitting. My niece's expression suggested she was counting to ten, a practice she'd adopted to keep her quick temper in check.

"Now, Mary Alice . . ." Judith soothed. "The ladies of Timber Coulee have pledged to send one hundred pairs of socks to our boys in France by Christmas. Surely we can find a way to combine our patriotic duties?"

"Patriotic duties?" Mary Alice's thin lips curved in a cold smirk. "Some might say our first duty is sending able-bodied young men to fight, not hiding them away in safe and easy jobs."

The knitting needles in Molly's hands stilled completely. I leaned forward, hoping to prevent the brewing argument, but Beatrice Fairmont beat me to it.

"Now see here." Beatrice's needles flashed as she gestured with them. "My Henry's serving as a field medic. Are you suggesting that's less patriotic than carrying a rifle?"

"Of course not," Mary Alice's voice dripped honey over steel, "but surely you see the difference between medical service and *true* combat? Besides, Henry isn't a real medic. He drives an ambulance. Anyone can drive these days. It's hardly the same as being shot at in the trenches, is it?"

Beatrice's face flushed crimson. "My son is bringing wounded men off the battlefield under enemy fire! How dare you suggest—"

"Mary Alice, leave her alone," Molly snapped. "You have some nerve, saying those things."

"Ladies, please!" Judith rapped that infernal baton sharply against the music stand. I was about ready to break that thing in two. "This is neither the time nor the place—"

But once Mary Alice got going, even those behemoth land machines the Brits were calling "tanks" couldn't stop her. She wheeled on Molly, completely ignoring Judith's attempt at intervention. "And that trumpeter of yours,

Molly Mulroney. Playing Sousa marches while real soldiers die? I'm certain it's very . . . entertaining."

The color drained from Molly's face. Her beau, Clarence Butterworth, was serving as a musician in a military band, using his considerable talent as a trumpeter to boost troop morale. Before she could respond, I glanced again at the sad-looking girl in the soprano section. Tears were now streaming silently down her face.

If only Sarah were here. How many times over the last few years had that thought pricked my heart? Sarah would have known exactly how to defuse this situation—she'd always been the peacemaker of the group.

"That's quite enough." I shot to my feet, surprising even myself. "We're all doing what we can for the war effort. Some knit, some sing, some serve overseas in whatever capacity they're assigned. Belittling others' contributions serves no one, especially not our boys in France."

For just a moment, as Mary Alice adjusted her music, I caught a flicker of something unexpected on her face—weariness, perhaps, or worry—before her usual imperious mask slipped back into place. It reminded me that even the most difficult people carried burdens of their own.

Judith seized the opportunity. "Exactly right, Amanda. Now, let's continue with measure twenty-seven."

The remainder of the rehearsal passed in strained politeness. Mary Alice sang her solo with technical perfection and emotional frigidity. Beatrice's needles clicked with military precision, her back ramrod straight. Molly looked ready to spit nails, and the dark-haired girl sniffled. When at last we finished, Judith dismissed us with unusual haste, clearly eager to end the tense gathering.

"Remember, we rehearse again on Thursday." She sounded less than delighted at the prospect.

As we gathered our things, Molly made her way to the sad young lady, who was dabbing at her eyes with a handkerchief. They spoke in hushed tones, heads close together. The girl nodded at whatever Molly was saying.

"Everything all right?" I asked when my niece joined me.

"That's Viola Thornton," she explained quietly.

"Oh, the Thornton girl," I said. "I thought she looked familiar. My, she's grown up since the days when she took clarinet lessons."

"Her brother's been serving overseas, and—well, I'll explain later."

My heart sank. "Poor thing. And then to sit through Mary Alice's tirade about who's serving properly."

"I told her I'd walk her home." Molly set her knitting basket on a shelf. "Her parents are beside themselves, and she could use someone to talk to who understands what it's like to worry about someone over there."

I nodded. "Of course. You run along. I'll close up here."

"Thanks, Aunt Amanda." Molly squeezed my hand. "And thank you for standing up to Mary Alice. Someone needed to put her in her place."

As Molly gently guided Viola toward the door, their heads bent together in conversation, Heidi appeared at my side, her expression troubled.

"That was unpleasant," she said. "I'm almost sorry I dragged you into this."

"Don't worry." I watched Mary Alice gather her things with imperious efficiency, pointedly ignoring Beatrice standing nearby. "Something tells me things would have been unpleasant whether I'd been here or not."

"Shall I see you on Thursday?"

"I shall look forward to it," I said through clenched teeth, meaning not a word.

Mary Alice approached me as the others filed out, Mildred hovering anxiously at her shoulder. "Miss Parrish, might Mildred and I stay behind for a short while? Since I won't be here Thursday, I need to work on that solo passage, and with how busy I am with important war work, tonight might be our only opportunity."

Had she adopted "important war work" as her personal slogan? I hesitated, glancing at Mildred, whose face was a portrait of conflicted emotions. Her nod was almost imperceptible.

"Of course," I said. "Just lock up when you've finished. Mildred, you have a key."

"Thank you," Mary Alice replied with uncharacteristic politeness. "We won't be long. Come along, Mildred."

Mildred murmured her thanks as well, not quite meeting my eyes. She hesitated.

"Don't be angry with Mary Alice," she whispered. "She doesn't mean to come across the way she does. She can be . . . demanding, but she's scrupulously honest. She only wants what's best for . . . for everyone."

With that mysterious comment, she retreated to the rehearsal room, pulling the curtain shut behind her.

I tidied the shop, straightening displays and putting away the tea service I'd set out for the choir members. The silence from the rehearsal room was curious—I heard no piano, no singing, only the occasional murmur of voices. Whatever they were discussing, it certainly wasn't Mary Alice's solo.

Moxie, who had been dozing on the counter, suddenly sat up, his ears perked forward, and leaped to the floor. His orange fur bristled along his spine as he stared intently at a dark corner behind the cello display.

"Oh, no. Don't tell me we have mice again!" I glared at my feline companion. "Aren't you supposed to take care of that sort of thing?"

Moxie's tail swished back and forth in agitation, but he pressed himself against my ankles. Mice made him anxious.

I sighed. It had been a long day, and my mystery novel awaited. "Aren't you the original scaredy-cat? Well, come on, let's go home. I'm too tired to deal with this now. We can set some traps tomorrow." I gathered my purse and coat, ready to call it a night.

"I'm leaving now," I called toward the rehearsal room. "Don't forget to lock up."

A muffled response came from behind the closed curtain—Mary Alice's voice, too indistinct to make out the words, but acknowledging enough to satisfy me. Then a loud sneeze erupted.

"Gesundheit," I called out automatically, amused by the satisfaction of using a German expression after Mary Alice's thinly veiled anti-German comments earlier. Nothing like a little linguistic rebellion to brighten my evening.

No response came, but Moxie meowed at the door, clearly eager to leave. As I turned the key in the lock, I had the oddest feeling of being watched. I glanced back over my shoulder, but saw only familiar shadows—instruments standing like silent sentinels, sheet music neatly arranged, the rehearsal room curtain closed.

With a shrug, I scooped up Moxie and stepped outside, locking the door behind me, determined that nothing more would stand between me and my date with Sherlock Holmes.

Chapter Three

The next morning, a steady rain pattered against the front windows of Mountain Melodies, giving the shop a cozy atmosphere even as it likely kept away customers. I hummed softly as I replaced the harmonica display with a new shipment of Victrola records. "Over There" was selling briskly these days, along with "Keep the Home Fires Burning" and "Pack Up Your Troubles." Songs of hope and homecoming—exactly what our worried town needed.

The door blew open and Molly breezed in, carrying an umbrella in one hand and a metal vacuum flask in the other.

"Good morning." She set the flask on the counter. "Mrs. Wasserman sends her regards and a sprinkle of cinnamon in your coffee."

"Bless that woman." I pulled two white china mugs from a shelf and poured the contents of the flask, inhaling the spicy aroma. "You're bright-eyed for someone who came home so late last night. I'm sorry I didn't wait up."

Molly shook out her wet umbrella and set it next to the door, then took her work smock from the wall peg and slipped it over her blouse. "I'm glad you didn't. I got home later than expected." She shot me a sideways glance. "You needn't worry about me, you know."

"I know. I just can't help it sometimes." The tear-streaked face of the girl from choir practice came to mind. "How is Viola doing?"

Molly's expression clouded as she stepped behind the counter. "Not well. Her family's in quite a state."

She busied herself organizing receipt slips, carefully straightening the already-neat stack. When she finally spoke, her voice was low.

"Her parents received a letter yesterday—very official-looking, on military letterhead. It said her brother Edward has run up gambling debts while stationed in France. Five hundred dollars' worth." She looked up, blue eyes wide. "Aunt Amanda, that's more than Mr. Thornton makes in three months at the mill."

I frowned. "Since when does the army concern itself with soldiers' personal debts?"

"That's just it. The letter claims he's being held in some kind of military detention facility until the debts are paid.

It says if his parents want to keep him out of a military prison, they need to wire the money to an account in Chicago."

"That doesn't sound right." I set down my coffee cup. "Surely the army has better things to do in the middle of a war than act as a collection agency for gambling debts."

"The Thorntons don't know what to think. They're beside themselves with worry. Mr. Thornton's talking about mortgaging their house."

"Has Viola shown the letter to anyone else? Someone who might know military procedures?"

Molly shook her head. "They're too embarrassed. The Thorntons are so proud of Edward—they don't want anyone to know he might be in trouble. That's why Viola was crying at rehearsal. She hadn't meant to tell anyone, but Mary Alice's comments about who was serving properly just . . ." She trailed off, anger flashing across her face. Her lightning-quick temper had worsened since Clarence's enlistment.

"Speaking of Mary Alice," I said, hoping to lighten the mood, "that was quite a performance she gave last night. And I don't mean her solo."

"Malice, you mean." Molly's lips quirked into a small smile.

"Malice?"

"That's what I call her in my head. Mary Alice, Malice. Fits her perfectly, don't you think?"

I laughed in spite of myself. "Molly Mulroney, that's unkind."

"But accurate." She took a stack of records from me and arranged them on the display. "The way she talked about Clarence, as if playing in the military band is somehow shirking duty . . . she hasn't the foggiest notion what she's talking about. The military has used music to signal the troops and lift their spirits for hundreds of years."

"Thousands. Think of the choir that went ahead of Jehoshaphat's army in the Bible. Anyway, don't let her get under your skin. That's exactly what she wants."

"I know. It's just . . ." Molly sighed, her shoulders slumping slightly. "Clarence's last letter said they're sending the band closer to the front lines now. To boost morale. They play in field hospitals, too."

My heart tightened. I hadn't known that. "Then he's every bit as much in danger as any other soldier."

"Yes, and he's doing something that actually helps those poor boys who are wounded or frightened. Music heals the soul. You know that better than anyone."

I nodded, thinking of the many times I'd seen music work its quiet magic. Even so, war was as unpredictable as it was terrifying. "And *you* know he's on my prayer list.

Every morning and every night." It was a small comfort, perhaps, but my faith had sustained me through my own dark times. The Lord had carried me when I couldn't walk on my own after Sarah's death. Now I would petition Him for Clarence's safety and Molly's peace of mind.

"Thank you," she whispered, her voice hoarse with unshed tears.

I pulled myself together. "Back to the situation at hand, remember that Mary Alice Wellington has made a lot of enemies over the years with that sharp tongue of hers. Try not to take it personally."

"I try not to." Molly shelved the last record and turned to face me. "But sometimes I wonder how you stand it. Especially since . . ."

"Since what?"

"Since you obviously don't enjoy singing with the choir. I could tell from your face last night. You love music of all kinds, but not this."

I sighed, closing the cash register drawer a bit harder than necessary. "It's hard to explain."

"Because of Sarah?"

I looked up sharply. "What do you know about Sarah?"

"Only what Heidi mentioned—that you used to sing together. And that she was Sheriff Holcomb's wife."

Sarah's name and James's in the same sentence still had the power to unsettle me, even after three years. I moved to the window display, needlessly adjusting record albums.

"Yes," I finally said. "Sarah and I sang together in the choir for years. She had a beautiful alto voice—much better than mine. We were always paired together for duets."

"What happened to her?" Molly asked gently.

"Typhoid." The single word couldn't possibly convey the devastation of that winter, when a number of people fell ill and a few never recovered, including Sarah. "Three years ago. It was quick. Too quick for anyone to even say goodbye properly."

Molly was quiet for a moment. "And that's why you stopped singing? Because it reminded you of her?"

"Singing was our favorite activity in common," I said simply. "We'd practice at her house—she had a lovely piano—and James would pretend to be annoyed by our caterwauling, as he called it. But sometimes I'd catch him in the doorway, just listening. After she died, all the joy went out of it."

Understanding dawned in Molly's eyes. "For him. And for you."

I turned away to dust an already immaculate violin display.

"Is that what's standing between you and Sheriff Holcomb?" she asked. "I've seen the way he looks at you. And the way you look at him when you think no one's watching."

Heat rose to my cheeks. "Molly, really. The sheriff and I are friends."

"Friends who can barely look each other in the eye? Who find excuses to be in the same place but never actually talk? Who—"

"That's enough." I turned to face her, finding compassion rather than teasing in her expression. "James hasn't . . . he hasn't gotten over Sarah. I'm not certain he ever will."

"And you feel guilty," she said softly. "About your feelings for him."

I stared at my niece. When had she become so perceptive? "It feels disloyal, somehow," I admitted. "To her memory. Sarah was my dearest friend, and James was hers, heart and soul."

"But she's been gone three years, right? Do you really think she'd want both of you to be alone forever?"

I'd asked myself the same question countless times, especially on quiet evenings when the emptiness of my house felt most acute. "It's not that simple."

"Maybe it could be," Molly suggested. "If you both stopped tiptoeing around each other and actually talked."

"We do talk."

"About the weather. Or shop security. Or town business." She picked up Moxie, who had wandered in from the back room, and cuddled him against her chest. "When was the last time you talked about anything that mattered?"

The door burst open, making us both start. Mr. Phillips from the post office stood in the doorway, his expression somber as he carefully removed his hat. My heart plummeted at the sight of the yellow envelope in his hand. I instinctively reached for Molly's arm as she stiffened beside me.

"Mr. Phillips," I managed, my voice barely above a whisper. The words *telegram* and *Clarence* hung unspoken in the air between us.

Molly's face had gone ghostly pale. "Is that—" Her voice caught, unable to finish the question.

Mr. Phillips looked confused for a moment, then his eyes widened in understanding. "Oh! Heavens, no!" He shook his head vigorously. "No, no, nothing like that, Miss Mulroney. I'm just here about some violin strings and to deliver a note to you, Miss Parrish."

The relief that washed over us was so powerful I had to steady myself against the counter. Molly pressed a trembling hand to her heart.

"I'm sorry to have given you such a fright." Contrition colored his face. "These days, I should know better than to look so serious when I enter a shop where someone has a loved one overseas."

"It's quite all right," I assured him, though my heart was still racing. "We're just a bit on edge these days. Now, what can we do for you?"

His cheerful demeanor returned. "I'm checking on that special order of violin strings. My Evelyn's driving me to distraction with her complaints about that broken E string."

"Just arrived yesterday. Sorry it took so long to get here." I moved to help him, grateful for the mundane business that would help settle my nerves. "Molly, would you check the storeroom for the new rosin we ordered? I think it might have come in the same shipment."

Molly still looked a bit shaken as she disappeared into the back.

As she left, Mr. Phillips handed me the envelope. "Sheriff Holcomb said he wanted you to have it before the council meeting tonight. I'd told him I'd be paying you a call."

My fingers tingled as I took the envelope, recognizing James's neat handwriting on the front. Just my name—"Amanda"—without "Miss Parrish" or any other formality.

"Thank you." I tucked it into my pocket, my earlier fear replaced by a different kind of quickened heartbeat. "Now, about those strings . . ."

As I wrapped Mr. Phillips's purchase, I was acutely aware of the letter in my pocket. What could James want that couldn't wait until the council meeting? Perhaps it was about the music for the war bonds fundraiser.

Or perhaps, a small voice whispered, it was something more personal.

Either way, I'd have to wait to find out. Molly would be back any moment, and I'd had quite enough personal conversation for one morning. Some things were better left unexamined—like why my heart raced at the sight of James's handwriting, or why, after three years, I still couldn't bring myself to sing the songs Sarah had loved.

And especially why, despite all my protestations, I found myself looking forward to seeing Sheriff James Holcomb at tonight's meeting.

A piercing shriek from the back room shattered my reverie. Mr. Phillips jumped, nearly dropping his package.

"Good heavens!" he exclaimed. "What was that?"

I forced a laugh, though my heart had leapt to my throat. "Molly must have seen a mouse. We've had a few come calling." I glanced around the shop floor. "Where is that cat when we need him?"

Mr. Phillips released a nervous chuckle. "Well, I hope she takes care of it before my Evelyn comes in for her lesson. That girl's more afraid of mice than she is of her arithmetic teacher."

Before I could respond, Molly emerged from the stockroom, a small wooden box of rosin clutched in her hands. Her face was ashen, all color drained away. She moved like someone in a dream, her steps uncertain.

"I found the . . . the rosin." She spoke barely above a whisper.

Something was very wrong. I'd seen that look before—on soldiers returning from the Spanish-American War, on families receiving telegrams from the front.

"Here you are, Mr. Phillips." I plucked a cake of rosin from the box in Molly's trembling hands. "Please give this to Evelyn with my compliments. It's on the house—to thank you both for your patience with our order."

He uttered a mild protest, but I was already ushering him toward the door, my hand at his elbow.

"No, I insist. Do tell her to let me know how the new strings work out. Good day, Mr. Phillips!"

The moment the door closed behind him, I crossed to Molly's side, took the box of rosin, and set it on the counter. "Molly? What is it? What's happened?"

She moved to the door, fastened the deadbolt, and flipped the Open sign to Closed. Her movements were mechanical, her eyes unfocused.

She swallowed hard, her gaze finally meeting mine. "You'd better come with me."

A cold dread settled in my stomach as I followed her to the back room. The air seemed to thicken with each step, making it harder to breathe. At the doorway, she paused, her hand gripping the frame as if for support.

"I went to check the third shelf for the rosin, like you asked." Her voice sounded oddly flat. "But I heard something—a kind of thump—coming from behind the instrument cases."

I peered past her into the room. Nothing seemed amiss at first glance—the upright piano stood against the wall, sheet music stacked neatly on shelves, and chairs arranged in rows where the choir had sat just yesterday.

"I thought maybe Moxie had knocked something over," Molly continued. "So I went to look, and that's when I . . ." She gestured weakly toward the far corner, where tall cabinets held our inventory of larger instruments.

I stepped around her and moved deeper into the room. As I approached the cabinets, my foot caught on something soft. I looked down.

Mary Alice Wellington lay sprawled on the floor, her arms flung wide as if in one final, dramatic gesture. Her eyes were open, staring sightlessly at the ceiling. Around her neck, pulled tight, was a length of olive-green yarn.

I slapped a hand over my mouth, stifling a cry. The room took a sickening tilt before righting itself. I forced myself to look closer, to take in the terrible tableau before me.

Mary Alice's face was contorted in surprise or fear, her features purpled by the yarn cinched tightly around her throat. Her hat lay a few feet away, its decorative feather now bent at an awkward angle. One of her hands still clutched a sheet of music, crumpled in her final struggle.

But it was what lay across her chest that made my blood run cold: a pair of knitting needles, arranged in the shape of a cross.

"The yarn," Molly whispered from behind me. "It's just like—"

"I know." Unlike the color of the ball that had tumbled from Heidi's bag yesterday—the same color that most the women were using for their soldiers' socks—the yarn around Mary Alice's neck matched the yarn in Molly's own knitting basket. Clarence was allergic to wool, so Molly knitted his socks of a cotton yarn that was a different shade of green than the woolen yarn used by most of the women.

"Did you take it home with you last night?"

"No. I know a lot of the ladies work on their knitting at home, but I never do. I just leave mine here in the shop so I don't forget it on rehearsal nights."

"So anyone could have used it," I murmured, more to myself than to Molly. "Or purchased another skein just like it."

A distant part of my mind—the part that wasn't frozen in horror—noticed other details. Mary Alice's reticule lay open beside her, its contents spilled across the floor. Sheet music from several folders was scattered about, as if someone had been searching through them. And the piano bench had been moved, its angle all wrong compared to where it had stood during last night's rehearsal.

"We need to call the sheriff." My voice sounded foreign to my own ears. "Don't touch anything."

I turned to look at my niece, whose face had gone from white to gray. "Molly," I said gently, "did you touch anything when you found her?"

She shook her head. "Only the doorframe and the rosin box. And then I screamed and came straight to you."

"Good. That's good." I took her arm and guided her back toward the front of the shop. "Go to the telephone and call the sheriff's office. Tell them . . ." I swallowed hard.

"Tell them there's been a death at Mountain Melodies. Tell them to come quickly."

As Molly moved woodenly toward the candlestick telephone on the counter, a soft thump from the stockroom made us both freeze. A moment later, Moxie sauntered out, his orange fur bristling, eyes wide and wary. He paused at the sight of us, then darted for the display window.

"Where were you when we needed you?" I murmured, the irrational thought floating through my shocked mind that if only the cat had been doing his duty, he might have somehow prevented this horror.

But that was nonsense, of course. Nothing could have saved Mary Alice Wellington from whoever had decided that her final performance had come to its end.

Who among us had hated Mary Alice enough to silence her forever—and why had they arranged those knitting needles in such a deliberate, accusing way?

Chapter Four

I stood by the shop window as James's deputies strung a rope across the entrance with a sign reading "Official Investigation—No Entry." The morning customers would be disappointed, but that seemed the least of my worries now.

I shivered in spite of the warm day. Inside, the shop had transformed from my sanctuary into a crime scene. Deputy Peterson, a serious young man with sandy hair, was in the stockroom, taking photographs of Mary Alice's body with a bulky camera. Another deputy was carefully examining the door locks and windows for signs of forced entry. James approached me, his expression grave and his professional demeanor firmly in place. Only the tightness around his eyes betrayed any personal feelings. "I have some questions, if you're up to it."

I nodded, clasping my clammy hands to keep them from trembling. Molly sat on a stool at the sales counter, her face still ashen. Moxie had curled up on her lap, keeping a wary eye on the deputies.

"Did you know there's a small window open in the stockroom?"

"That's Moxie's window. It's how he gets in and out whenever he wants."

"I see. Well, it's scarcely big enough for an intruder to gain access, but you might want to keep it closed nonetheless. Though you probably won't, for Moxie's sake."

He knew me well.

We sat on a couple of folding chairs. "When did you last see Mrs. Wellington alive?" James flipped open a notebook.

"Last night at choir practice. Around nine o'clock, when everyone was leaving." I frowned, trying to recall the sequence of events.

"Did everyone leave together?" he asked.

"Most did. But Mary Alice asked Mildred—she's our accompanist—to stay behind to work on her solo. Said she needed the extra practice."

"And did you see them leave?"

"No." At last, a fact I was sure about. "I told them they could stay. Mildred has had a key for years. She teaches piano lessons here sometimes. I asked her to lock up when they were finished, and I left."

James quirked an eyebrow. "So Mildred Abernathy and Mary Alice Wellington were the last people in the shop, to your knowledge?"

"Yes."

"I'll need to speak with her." James made a note. "Does she live nearby?"

"Birch Street, the little white cottage with blue shutters."

"Excuse me just a moment." James stood and conferred with Deputy Miller. Then the deputy left, and James returned to his seat.

"And after you left Mildred and Mrs. Wellington here, what did you do?"

"I went home. To my house. Which is just around the corner. As you know." Shock and distress were causing me to babble.

"Alone?"

"Yes. Molly had gone to walk Viola Thornton home."

James turned to Molly. "How long were you gone, Miss Mulroney?"

Molly looked up, her fingers absently stroking Moxie's fur as the cat purred in her lap. "I'm not certain exactly. Two hours, perhaps? The Thorntons live on Maple Street, and Viola was vexed. I stayed to talk with her for a while."

James made another note. I glanced at Molly's face. Maple Street was only a ten-minute walk from the shop. Even allowing time for conversation, two hours seemed excessive. A small, unwelcome doubt flickered in my mind, which I immediately tried to dismiss. This was Molly, for heaven's sake.

"Maple Street is in the opposite direction from your house. Did you pass Mountain Melodies on your way home?"

Molly nodded.

"When you passed the shop, did you notice anything unusual? Any sign someone might have been here?"

"No, sir. The shop was dark."

"Was the door locked?"

"I don't know. I didn't try to open it." She cocked her head. "Why would I?"

"Did you see anyone else near the shop? Mrs. Abernathy or Mrs. Wellington leaving, perhaps?"

Molly shook her head. "No one."

"What time was this, approximately?"

"Around eleven, I think."

James made another note. "So if they were still working on the solo at that time, the shop wouldn't have been dark."

I hadn't considered that. "Unless they were in the back room. The window there faces the alley, not the street."

"And this morning?" James turned back to me. "When did you open up?"

"Around half past seven, as usual. Everything was exactly as I'd left it. No signs of disturbance, no broken windows, nothing missing that I could see." I paused. "Until Molly found . . . her."

"You mentioned Mrs. Abernathy has a key. Anyone else, besides you and Molly?"

"Several people have keys."

"How so?"

"Well, other music teachers, so they can hold private lessons here after hours. Rose MacTavish taught violin before she had her baby. And I gave a key to Judith Hensley a while back. She needed to be able to lock up after I . . . after I quit the choir and Molly hadn't joined yet." I hesitated. "But surely none of those people would—"

"We'll need to account for all existing keys." James's tone was neutral. "Do you know of anyone who might have had a grudge against Mrs. Wellington?"

"Who didn't?" A humorless snort escaped me before I could stop it. "Sorry, that was unkind. But Mary Alice had a talent for making enemies." Molly's words came back to me. *I call her Malice in my head.*

"Anyone specific?" James prompted. "Anyone who might have been angry enough to do this?"

I thought of the scene at rehearsal, Mary Alice's cutting remarks about soldiers' service. "Beatrice Fairmont was furious with her last night. Not only do those two seem to have an ongoing rivalry concerning who gets to sing solos, but Mary Alice insulted her son's military service. Poor Viola Thornton was in tears." I glanced at my niece. Mary Alice hadn't been kind to Molly about Clarence, either. But I didn't mention that to James.

"Half the choir was annoyed with her," Molly added. "She was needling everyone about their 'patriotic duty' and making snide comments about which military roles really mattered."

James scowled. "What prompted this discussion?"

"The knitting," I explained. "Mary Alice complained about the clicking of needles during rehearsal, and it spiraled from there."

"Knitting needles," James repeated, glancing back at the stockroom. "Like the ones crossed on her chest."

The air in the shop seemed heavy and stale. "It seems . . . deliberate. Like someone wanted to make a point."

"Or wanted to implicate the knitting circle," James murmured.

Deputy Peterson approached and spoke quietly to James. He nodded and turned back to us.

"I'll need a complete list of everyone who attended choir practice last night," he said. "And I'd like to speak with each of them."

"Of course," I said. "Judith would have the official attendance sheet, but I can tell you most of who was there."

As I listed the choir members, James wrote each name in his meticulous handwriting. When I finished, he asked, "Have you spoken to Mrs. Abernathy this morning?"

"No," I replied. "I had no cause to. Why?"

James's expression was carefully neutral. "She was the last person known to be with Mrs. Wellington. We need her statement."

Deputy Peterson returned to James's side. "Sheriff, you might want to see this."

"Excuse me." James followed his deputy to a quiet corner. They conferred in low voices, James's expression growing more troubled. When he looked up, his gaze met mine briefly before sliding away. He walked toward the back room, and I fought the urge to follow him.

A few minutes later, James emerged holding something in a handkerchief. He approached slowly, his expression carefully controlled.

"Miss Parrish, do you recognize this?" He opened the handkerchief slightly, revealing a small silver thimble with a distinctive floral pattern and the initials "M. M."

My blood ran cold as I realized what those initials stood for.

"Molly Mulroney," James said softly, confirming my fear.

"That's impossible," I blurted. "Molly would never—"

"Aunt Amanda?" Molly had approached, her brow furrowed with confusion. "What's wrong?"

James turned to her, his expression softening slightly. "Miss Mulroney, did you misplace your thimble last night?"

Molly stared at the thimble, her face draining of color. "No. Why?"

"This thimble was found next to the body."

"It looks like my thimble," she admitted, "and those are my initials. But I'd swear it was in my knitting basket last night when I left."

He glanced back toward the stockroom. "Deputy Peterson also found cotton knitting yarn around Mrs. Wellington's neck. The same color and type as the yarn you were using last night for your socks."

Molly paled further. "But everyone in the choir uses that color yarn. We have to use the same color for the soldiers' socks."

"Not quite the same," I interjected, desperate to defend my niece. "Molly uses a cotton yarn for Clarence's socks because of his sensitive skin. She special-ordered it from Johnston's Dry Goods."

Instead of helping, my words seemed to make things worse. James's expression grew more troubled.

"So this particular yarn would only be found in your knitting basket?" he asked Molly.

"I . . . I suppose so," she stammered. "But I didn't—"

"Miss Mulroney," James interrupted, his voice regretful but firm, "I'm afraid I need you to come down to the station to answer some questions."

"James!" I protested, but he held up a hand.

"Just questions, Amanda. For now." His eyes held mine, and I saw the conflict there—the sheriff doing his duty versus the man who had once been like family. "But I can't ignore evidence."

"I'll come too," I said immediately.

James shook his head. "I need to speak with you separately. Deputy Peterson will stay with you until I'm ready."

As James led my trembling niece toward the door, Molly looked back at me, her eyes wide with fear. "Aunt Amanda, I didn't do this. I swear I didn't."

"I know," I called after her. "Don't worry. We'll sort this out."

But as the door closed behind them, I wasn't certain whom I was trying to convince—Molly or myself. The evidence seemed damning: the thimble with her initials, the special yarn, her unaccounted time after walking Viola home. And Mary Alice's cruel comments about Clarence would give her motive, on top of her general dislike for the woman. *I call her Malice in my head.*

Yet I knew Molly. She might have a temper, but she wasn't capable of such calculated violence. Was someone trying to frame her?

Chapter Five

The brass bell above the door of Mountain Melodies had been silenced, wrapped in black crepe by Molly that morning. "Out of respect," she'd said, though I suspected she simply couldn't bear its cheerful jingle so soon after finding Mary Alice's body. After being questioned at the sheriff's office, she'd been released. For the time being, anyway. Any evidence pointing to her was purely circumstantial. But we both knew she wouldn't be completely cleared of suspicion until the true culprit was discovered and arrested.

Three days had passed since the murder. The shop had reopened—James's deputies had finished their on-site examination by the second day—but a somber mood hung in the air like the lingering notes of a funeral dirge. Customers spoke in hushed voices, their eyes darting to the back room as if expecting to see Mary Alice's ghost emerge from behind the curtain.

Sheriff Holcomb had questioned me twice more, his professional demeanor never slipping, even when asking about Molly's whereabouts the night of the murder. I'd told him everything I knew, fighting the unworthy suspicion that my niece wasn't being entirely forthcoming about her two-hour absence.

A light rain tapped against the shop windows, softening the edges of what had been a cold spring day. I'd spent hours helping a young mother select the perfect beginner's violin for her daughter, grateful for the distraction of normal business. But now, with the clock showing half past four and no customers in sight, my mind returned to the dark thoughts I'd been pushing away.

Who had killed Mary Alice Wellington? And why in my shop, of all places?

The door banged open.

I looked up, expecting Molly's return from her errand to the post office. Instead, Sheriff James Holcomb stood in the doorway, water droplets clinging to the brim of his hat.

"Amanda." His voice was soft but formal. "Do you have a moment?"

My heart quickened despite my best efforts to remain composed. "Of course. Would you like some coffee? I just made a fresh pot."

"That would be welcome. Thank you."

I busied myself with pouring two cups from the electric percolator at the back of the shop, aware of him removing his hat, running a hand through his slightly damp hair. When I returned, he and I stood on either side of the sales counter, across from each other.

"This isn't a social call, is it?" I set a cup before him.

"I'm afraid not." He took a sip, meeting my eyes over the rim. "Is Molly here?"

"Not at the moment. I sent her to the post office."

"Good. I wanted to speak with you privately, before Deputy Peterson files his official report."

Something in his tone made my stomach tighten. I set my own cup down untouched.

"You've identified a suspect."

"We've narrowed our focus to three primary suspects," he corrected gently.

I waited, dreading what would come next.

"Beatrice Fairmont, Mildred Abernathy, and . . ." he hesitated, his professional mask slipping for just a moment, "Molly."

Though I'd feared as much, hearing him say it aloud nauseated me. "Molly? James, that's absurd."

"Is it?" His voice remained gentle, but his eyes held mine steadily. "She had a public argument with Mary Alice the evening she died, and she had a strong motive to defend her fiancé's honor."

"Having an argument isn't the same as committing murder!"

"No, it isn't. But it establishes motive." He sighed, setting down his cup. "Amanda, I don't want to believe Molly could do such a thing. But I have to follow the evidence."

"What evidence?" I demanded.

He cleared his throat. "Setting aside the unique nature of the yarn for a moment, the knitting needles positioned on Mary Alice's chest match what most of the choir knitters use, yes. But Deputy Peterson has interviewed every member of the choir. Many of the ladies simply wouldn't have had the physical strength required."

"And you think Molly did?"

"Whoever strangled Mary Alice Wellington had strong hands and arms." His tone remained measured, factual. "Molly is young, physically fit, and as you told me yourself, she's been playing violin since childhood."

I stared at him in disbelief. "So now being a violinist makes her a murderer?"

"It gives her the physical capability. That, combined with motive, opportunity, and . . ." He hesitated again.

"And what?"

"And the unaccounted time after rehearsal." He met my gaze directly. "According to Viola Thornton's statement, Molly left the Thornton home no later than a quarter to ten. Yet she didn't return home until after eleven."

A wave of cold dread washed over me. I'd sensed there was something off about Molly's timeline, but I'd pushed the thought away, ashamed of doubting her.

"That doesn't mean anything," I protested, though my voice lacked conviction. "She could have gone anywhere. For a walk, to the church . . ."

"In the dark? Alone?" James shook his head. "That would be remarkably foolish, especially for a young woman as sensible as Molly."

"Then she must have had a good reason."

"I hope so." James's voice softened. "I've asked her directly, Amanda. She says she can't account for that time."

"Can't or won't?"

"She says she doesn't remember exactly where she went or what she did. That she was troubled and wandering." He leaned forward. "That's not like Molly. You know that."

I did know. Molly had always been methodical, precise about her whereabouts. If she'd truly "wandered" for over an hour, it would be the first time in her life.

"There must be some explanation," I insisted.

"I hope there is." James's hand moved across the counter, as if he might reach for mine, then stopped. "I'm not approaching this lightly. But the evidence points to someone who argued with Mary Alice that night, who had the physical strength to overpower her, and who had access to the shop during the window of time when she was killed."

I took a deep breath, trying to quell the panic rising in my chest. "So what about Beatrice?"

"According to witnesses, she had an ongoing and very public rivalry with Mary Alice concerning who was the lead soprano."

"True. But hardly worth killing someone over."

"And they argued over remarks made by Mary Alice over Beatrice's son's military service."

"Also true." But was even that enough to push her over the edge? "And Mildred Abernathy?"

James's expression grew more serious. "The fact that we haven't been able to locate her is troubling, to say the least."

"But she's Mary Alice's cousin!"

"Second cousin," he corrected, "and family relationships don't preclude violence. In fact, they often provide the strongest motives."

"What possible motive could Mildred have?"

James consulted a small notebook. "According to several witnesses, Mary Alice had been critical of Mildred's playing recently. Called it 'sloppy' and 'uninspired' during recent rehearsals. Said the choir deserved better accompaniment."

I winced, remembering the exchange. "That was just Mary Alice being Mary Alice. She criticized everyone and demanded perfection, especially during her solo parts."

"Perhaps. But we won't know until we talk to her. And we can't talk to her if we can't find her." James turned a page in his notebook. "What troubles me most is the timing. Mary Alice is murdered, and the very next day, Mildred seemingly vanishes. It's suspicious."

I took a sip of my now-cooled coffee. "So you suspect Beatrice because she argued with Mary Alice about her son's service. You suspect Mildred because Mary Alice criticized her playing and now you can't find her."

"And she was the last person seen with Mary Alice," James prompted. "Don't forget that not-insignificant detail."

"And you suspect Molly because she defended Clarence and can't account for her time." I shook my head. "That's circumstantial at best."

"For now." His voice took on an edge I rarely heard. "But Deputy Peterson continues to interview witnesses. And we're looking into Mary Alice's other associates and relatives, too. If there's a pattern of conflict or trouble, we'll find it."

We stood facing each other across the counter, the space between us suddenly vast. I thought of Sarah, of how she would have hated to see us at odds like this.

"What happens now?" I struggled to keep my voice steady.

"Nothing immediately. We're still gathering evidence." He settled his hat carefully. "I came to you first, out of . . . professional courtesy."

Professional courtesy. Not friendship. Not the nameless, growing thing that had been between us since Sarah's death. Just courtesy, from the sheriff to a shopkeeper whose niece was under suspicion.

"I see."

"Amanda . . ." He hesitated, something unreadable in his eyes. "I hope we're wrong about all three of them. I truly do."

"You are." I drew myself up, summoning every ounce of dignity I possessed. "And I intend to prove it."

"Don't interfere with this investigation," he warned, his tone sharpening. "This isn't like the Lucas Baker case. A meddling amateur could do more harm than good."

"Amateur?" The word stung more than it should have. "Is that what I am to you, James? An amateur who meddles?"

"That's not what I meant."

"Isn't it?" I moved toward the door, opening it pointedly. "Thank you for the warning, Sheriff. Rest assured, I'll stay out of your way while you build your case against my innocent niece."

"Amanda, please."

"Good day, Sheriff Holcomb."

For a moment, I thought he might say more. Instead, he gave a curt nod and stepped out into the rain. He walked away, his normally straight shoulders slightly hunched against the weather, or perhaps against the weight of what had just passed between us.

Only when he turned the corner did I close the door, leaning against it as emotion washed over me. Anger, fear, hurt—all tangled together like the yarn that had ended Mary Alice's life.

Molly, a murderer? The mere thought was preposterous. My niece, who nursed injured birds back to health and wept over sad endings in novels. Who had once refused to kill a spider in the bathtub, insisting on capturing it in a jar and releasing it outside.

And Mildred? The woman who'd played for concerts, church services, weddings, and funerals for the past umpteen years without complaint? Who baked extra cookies for choir rehearsals "just in case someone needed a bit of sweetening"? I couldn't imagine her hands, which coaxed such lively music from the piano keys, tightening yarn around Mary Alice's throat.

No. Whatever happened that night, whoever had arranged those knitting needles in that ghastly cross, it wasn't Molly. And I highly doubted it was Mildred or even Beatrice, despite her very public rivalry with Mary Alice.

Which meant the real killer was still out there, perhaps watching as James focused his investigation on three innocent women.

I crossed to the counter and pulled out a fresh sheet of paper. At the top, I wrote "Suspects" and underlined it firmly. Below, I began listing names, starting with Beatrice Fairmont and Mildred Abernathy. But I left Molly's name off the list entirely.

I might not know who killed Mary Alice Wellington, but I knew who didn't. And I would prove it, with or without James Holcomb's approval.

Chapter Six

By the time Molly returned from the post office, cheeks flushed from the cool rain, I had filled an entire page with notes and questions.

"I'm back. Has it been busy?" She hung her wet coat on a peg.

I hastily tucked the paper beneath a ledger. "Not very," I said. "Did you manage to mail Clarence's package?"

"Yes, though Mr. Phillips says it might take longer than usual to reach Europe." She leaned against the counter, her damp hair curling around her face. "Is everything all right? You look a little peaked."

I mustered a weak smile. "Just tired. It's been a long day."

She studied me with the perceptiveness that sometimes made me forget how young she was. "Did something happen while I was gone?"

I hesitated, torn between shielding her and being honest. I opted for honesty.

"Sheriff Holcomb was here. He wanted to update me on the investigation."

Molly stiffened. "Did he mention me?"

The directness of her question caught me unawares. "Why would you ask that?"

"Because I'm not blind. I've seen how people look at me in town. I've heard the whispers." Her chin lifted slightly. "And I know Deputy Peterson has been asking all sorts of questions about me."

I abandoned all pretense of calm. "Molly, where were you after you left Viola's house that night?"

Her face paled. "I told you. I walked home."

"For over an hour?" I couldn't keep the edge from my voice. "It's a ten-minute walk from the Thorntons' to our house. Fifteen, at the most."

"I . . . I needed time to think." She looked away. "Viola was so distressed about her brother, and then all that business with Mary Alice at rehearsal . . . I just needed some air."

"So you wandered the streets alone? In the middle of the night?" I shook my head. "That's not like you, Molly."

"Well, maybe you don't know me as well as you think," she snapped, then immediately looked contrite. "I'm sorry. I didn't mean that."

"If there's something you're not telling me—"

"There isn't." She met my eyes directly. "I swear it, Aunt Amanda. I did not kill Mary Alice Wellington."

I studied her face, searching for any hint of deception. I found none.

"I believe you," I said firmly. "But James—Sheriff Holcomb—is building a case. He thinks you had motive and opportunity."

"Because I was angry about what she said about Clarence?" Molly laughed in disbelief. "Half the choir was angry with her that night!"

"Half the choir doesn't have unaccounted hours after rehearsal." I took her hands, feeling their strength—the violinist's strength that James had mentioned. "Molly, whatever happened during that time, whatever you did or didn't do, you need to tell me. I can't help you if I don't know the truth."

For a moment, something flickered in her eyes—hesitation, perhaps, or fear. Then she squeezed my hands.

"I've told you everything," she said quietly. "I was worried about Viola. I walked. I came home. And I discovered the next morning that Mary Alice was dead."

I wanted desperately to believe her. Needed to believe her.

"All right." I released her hands. "Then we'll just have to find out who really killed Mary Alice."

"We?"

"I'm not going to sit by while the sheriff builds a case against you." I moved back to the counter, pulling out the list I'd begun. "Someone in this town had reason enough to kill Mary Alice Wellington. Someone besides you or Mildred or, frankly, Beatrice Fairmont. And I intend to find out who."

Molly glanced at my list. "You're investigating? But Sheriff Holcomb—"

"Is convinced he already knows who did it." I could hear the bitterness in my voice. "So it's up to us to prove him wrong."

"Aunt Amanda . . ." Molly hesitated. "Are you doing this because you believe in my innocence, or because you're angry at the sheriff?"

The question stung with its accuracy. "Does it matter?"

"It does to me."

I met her gaze steadily. "I'm doing this because you're my family, and I know you couldn't have done this terrible thing. And yes, I'm also doing it because James Holcomb should know better than to accuse you without solid evidence."

A ghost of a smile touched her lips. "So it's personal."

"Very personal." I summoned a brittle smile in return. "Now, let's start with what we know about Mary Alice's last day alive."

Chapter Seven

At closing time, we put away our notes on the case and prepared for that evening's choir rehearsal.

"You're being ridiculous," I scolded myself as I arranged chairs. Molly had no reason to lie. No reason to harm Mary Alice. She was simply consoling a friend, and conversations about brothers and boyfriends in peril could certainly stretch on.

The back room had been scrubbed clean by deputies, but I could still see the outline of Mary Alice's body when I closed my eyes. The crossed knitting needles. The yarn pulled tight around her throat.

"Aunt Amanda?" Molly appeared in the doorway, a stack of sheet music in her arms. "Judith asked if we could set up the chairs in a circle tonight. She thinks it might be . . . comforting."

I nodded, pushing away the dark thoughts. "Of course. How many are we expecting?"

"Most everyone, I think. Though Mrs. Brown sent word she's too distraught to attend."

"Mrs. Brown barely knew Mary Alice. More likely she's missing because she's attending the Ladies' Aid meeting instead."

Molly gave me a measured look. "I think she's more scared than distraught. Everyone's frightened, and why not? Someone killed Mary Alice in our shop."

Our shop. The place that had always been my sanctuary now felt tainted, violated.

"I know." I softened my tone. "I'm sorry, Molly. I haven't been sleeping well."

"Neither have I." She set down the music and began arranging chairs. "Sheriff Holcomb asked me to come to the station this afternoon. For more questions."

My hands stilled on the hymnal I was shelving. "What kind of questions?"

"The same as before. When did I leave Viola's house? Did I come straight home? Did I see anyone on the way?" Her voice tightened. "He asked if I'd had any disagreements with Mary Alice before that night."

"That's standard procedure." I tried to sound reassuring. "He's asking everyone the same questions."

"I know. But it feels like . . ." She trailed off, biting her lip.

"Like he suspects you?" I finished gently.

"Like everyone suspects me." She looked down at her hands. "I've seen how people look at me in town. They know Mary Alice and I argued. They know my yarn was—" She broke off as the door swung open.

Judith Hensley bustled in, carrying her music case. Her normally cheerful face was drawn with fatigue. "Amanda, Molly, thank goodness you're here. I wasn't certain if—well, I wasn't certain about anything, to be honest."

Behind her came several other choir members, moving in tight clusters as if for protection. Heidi immediately came to my side, squeezing my arm in support.

"How are you holding up?" she whispered.

"As well as can be expected," I replied. "You?"

"Barely sleeping. I keep thinking about the time I was attacked in my own store. And how fortunate I was to survive. I also keep thinking about those knitting needles. Why would anyone do such a thing?"

Before I could respond, the door opened again. Sheriff Holcomb entered, followed by Deputy Peterson. The room fell silent.

"Ladies." James stood before us, his expression grave. "Thank you for your cooperation during this difficult time. I'll need to speak with a few more of you tonight, if you don't mind." He turned to Judith. "I hope we won't disrupt your rehearsal too much."

"Of course not, Sheriff." Judith's voice was steadier than her hands, which trembled as she fingered the flag pin on her lapel. "We can set up a space for you in the shop. Isn't that right, Amanda?"

"Of course." I busied myself with the final chair arrangements, aware of James's eyes on me. When I glanced up, he quickly looked away, but not before I caught a flicker of something in his expression—concern, perhaps, or maybe just professional scrutiny.

As the choir members filed in, their subdued demeanor tempered the room. The usual chatter was replaced by whispered conversations, nervous glances, tense postures. The community of women who had once found joy in music now huddled together in fear.

"Ladies." Judith brought the room to attention. "Before we begin, I thought we might have a moment of prayer for Mary Alice."

Heads bowed. In the silence, someone wept softly.

"Lord," Judith began, her voice gaining strength, "we come before you with heavy hearts, mourning the loss of our fellow chorister, Mary Alice Wellington. Though her voice has been silenced on earth, we trust it now joins the heavenly choir. Grant comfort to her family and friends, wisdom to those seeking justice, and peace to our troubled community. Amen."

"Amen," the room echoed.

As heads lifted, Beatrice Fairmont spoke up. "Sheriff, can you tell us anything more about what happened? We've heard all sorts of rumors."

James stepped forward, his posture straight, hands clasped behind his back. "I'm afraid I can't discuss details of an ongoing investigation, Mrs. Fairmont. What I can say is that we're pursuing every lead and interviewing everyone who might have information."

"Everyone who might have a motive, you mean," someone muttered.

James continued as if he hadn't heard. "In the meantime, I advise all of you to be vigilant. Lock your doors and windows. Try not to be alone, especially after dark."

A ripple of unease spread through the room.

"Do you think we're in danger?" Heidi squeaked, her voice small.

"We have no reason to believe the public at large is in danger," James replied. "But until we know more, caution is advisable."

The heavy silence that followed was broken by Judith clearing her throat. "I have one more announcement before we begin. As some of you may have heard, Mildred

Abernathy has been called away unexpectedly due to a family emergency in Seattle."

Surprised murmurs filled the room. Mildred was a fixture in our little community. Her sudden absence felt like another wound.

"When did this happen?" I blurted, unable to keep the surprise from my voice.

"She telephoned me early Tuesday morning," Judith replied. "Said she'd just received a telegram from her family and was leaving on the morning train. Barely had time to pack, poor thing. This was before any of us had heard about our dear Mary Alice. Except for you, of course, Amanda." She gave me the sort of pitying look one gives to victims of natural disasters.

James's face lit with interest, and I could almost see the professional wheels turning in his mind. "That was sudden, and explains why we've been unable to reach her at home," he remarked. "Did you see this telegram?"

Judith looked startled. "Well, no. She telephoned me about it. Why do you ask?"

"Just establishing a timeline." James's reply was smooth, though I could tell from the tightening around his eyes that Mildred's abrupt departure had heightened his investigative instincts.

"Fortunately," Judith continued, apparently oblivious to the sheriff's interest, "we've found a temporary replacement." She gestured toward the door, where my Debussy-loving customer from earlier in the week stood quietly. "Ladies, please welcome Eleanor Crawford. Some of you may have already met her around town these past few weeks. She's graciously agreed to step in as our accompanist until Mildred returns."

Eleanor stepped forward, acknowledging the subdued greetings with a dignified nod. Her navy dress was simple but well-tailored, and she carried herself with quiet confidence.

"Thank y'all for havin' me." Her voice carried through the room, melodious with an accent as thick as Georgia molasses. "I'm sorry it's under such distressin' circumstances."

"Mrs. Crawford is a journalist." Judith sounded awestruck, as if journalism were a career on a level with hunting lions in Africa or swinging on a trapeze in the circus. "She recently arrived in Timber Coulee to do research for a series of articles on how women in the West are supporting the war effort."

As Eleanor settled at the piano, beaming a sunny smile to all and sundry, I studied her with interest. There was something compelling about her—a sureness, an attitude of confidence as she arranged her music. For no clear reason, I took an immediate liking to her.

She sniffled and dabbed her eyes with a delicate lace handkerchief. "Don't mind me, y'all. This pollen is really gettin' to me."

Several women murmured in agreement. "It seems especially bad this year," Beatrice said. "I hope it won't affect our singing voices too terribly." She emitted a feeble cough to emphasize her point.

James touched Judith's elbow. "If you don't mind, we'll begin our interviews with Mrs. Fairmont."

Judith nodded, and Beatrice followed him out to the main shop, where Deputy Peterson had set up a small table and chairs.

"Let's start with warm-ups," Judith said, trying to inject normality into the abnormal situation. "And then we'll work on 'The Star-Spangled Banner.'"

Needles clicked as we warmed our voices. Eleanor's fingers moved across the keys with professional precision, drawing forth arpeggios. Her playing was different from Mildred's—more controlled, more nuanced. Where Mildred played with enthusiastic energy, Eleanor created delicate layers of sound, each note precisely placed.

Throughout the rehearsal, James called women away one by one. When my turn came, he led me to a quiet corner of the shop floor.

"I appreciate your cooperation, Miss Parrish," he began formally, though his eyes held a hint of the warmth I remembered from before tragedy had redrawn the lines of our relationship.

"Of course," I replied. "Anything to help."

He nodded, then lowered his voice. "What can you tell me about Mildred Abernathy's departure? Did she mention anything to you about a family emergency?"

I shook my head. "Nothing. I'm as surprised as you are."

"And you find the timing . . . interesting?" His even tone betrayed no emotion, no hint of what he might be thinking.

"Are you suggesting Mildred had something to do with Mary Alice's death?" I couldn't keep the incredulity from my voice. "They were cousins, James. Second cousins, but still family."

"Family disputes can be the most dangerous." He made a note in his book. "And the timing is suspicious—leaving town immediately after a murder. Especially since she was apparently the last person to see the victim alive."

"But Mildred and Mary Alice rarely quarreled, at least not publicly." I tried to recall any tension between them.

"They weren't particularly close, but they were cordial. Professional."

"Did Mildred have a key to the shop?"

"Yes, of course. I already told you that." A shiver ran down my arms as I realized the implication. "James, surely you don't think—"

"I'm considering all possibilities, Amanda." His use of my given name, so rare in professional settings, indicated how seriously he took this new development. "A woman is murdered in a locked building. Another woman with access to that building suddenly leaves town with barely a word to anyone. It merits investigation."

I couldn't argue with his logic, though my heart refused to accept Mildred as a murderer. "If you knew Mildred better, you'd know she couldn't hurt anyone, let alone her own cousin. She cries when she finds dead birds in her garden."

"People surprise us," he said simply. "Especially when pushed to extremes."

"What extremes?" I challenged. "What possible motive could Mildred have?"

James hesitated, then replied, "I'm not ready to speculate on that yet. But I will need to question her, and to do that, I need to find her."

I opened my mouth to defend Mildred further, then closed it. James was right—every possibility needed to be examined, no matter how unlikely it seemed to me.

"I should return to the rehearsal." I stood. "Is there anything else?"

James regarded me thoughtfully. "Just be observant, Amanda. Notice things. People often reveal more than they intend."

With that cryptic advice, he escorted me back to the rehearsal room.

When I returned to my seat, the group had stopped singing, but continued to knit as they listened to Eleanor play a soft, contemplative version of "Look Away, Dixieland." Her fingers danced across the keys with graceful assurance, drawing forth a melody that seemed to speak directly to our collective grief and fear. I wondered if the folk song held special significance for her.

As the song ended and the women gathered their things, I approached the piano. "That last piece was beautiful."

Eleanor looked up with a warm smile that crinkled the corners of her eyes. "Oh, thank you, sugar! Just a little arrangement of my own. Music has always been my way of sortin' through life's tangles."

"You're a composer as well as a pianist?"

"Bless your heart, I'm just a dabbler." She gave a self-deprecating laugh. "Nothin' worth publishin'. My mama always said I had more enthusiasm than talent, but it soothes my soul all the same."

"I'd love to hear more," I found myself saying. "Perhaps we could have tea sometime?"

"Now wouldn't that be lovely!" Her face lit up like a child receiving a birthday gift. "I'd enjoy that more than cream enjoys peaches. Saturday, perhaps? I hear there's a new tearoom on Elm Street. The ladies at the bank say their scones are divine."

"Perfect. I only work half a day on Saturdays. I close up at noon."

"Half past twelve, then?"

We left the rehearsal room together and entered the shop. Eleanor glanced toward James, who was concluding his final interview of the evening. "That poor man looks plumb exhausted. Do you think he'll find who did this terrible thing?"

"Sheriff Holcomb is very thorough."

"That's good to hear." She touched my arm gently. "A strong, dedicated lawman is a real blessin' to a community. Why, back home in Georgia, our sheriff couldn't find his own shadow at high noon!" She gave a musical laugh, then squeezed my hand. "Until Saturday, then."

"I look forward to it." This time, I meant it.

"And perhaps," she lowered her voice confidentially, "you might share a little more about Timber Coulee's families for my article? Especially those with loved ones overseas? I want to make certain their stories are told with the respect they deserve."

"I'd be happy to." Her dedication to honoring our community's sacrifices touched me.

As I watched her leave, her skirts swishing merrily around her ankles, I felt a small surge of hope. Perhaps this new friendship would be a bright spot in these dark days. Someone to talk to who wasn't directly involved in the snarled web of small-town relationships and long-held grudges.

Someone whose warm Southern charm and genuine interest in others' welfare reminded me why I'd fallen in love with small-town life in the first place. Someone who didn't remind me of Mary Alice's death.

But who did remind me, at least a little bit, of Sarah.

Later, as I locked up the shop, I found myself thinking of Mildred and her sudden departure. James's questions had planted a seed of doubt that I couldn't quite dismiss. Would Mildred really leave town without a word to anyone besides Judith? Without saying goodbye to any of the choir members she'd played for all these years?

It didn't seem like her. But then, murder didn't seem like *anyone* I knew in Timber Coulee.

And yet, someone I knew—perhaps someone who had been in this very room tonight—had strangled Mary Alice Wellington and arranged those knitting needles in a deliberate cross upon her chest.

The thought sent a chill through me as I made my final check of the windows and doors. Tomorrow, I would make some inquiries about Mildred's departure. Not because I suspected her—I couldn't bring myself to believe Mildred capable of such violence—but because her absence felt wrong, somehow. Like another piece of the puzzle that didn't quite fit.

And in my experience, when pieces didn't fit, it usually meant someone was trying to force them into the wrong place.

Chapter Eight

On Saturday morning, leaving Molly in charge of Mountain Melodies, I paid a visit to Frocks & Frills, the ladies' dress shop owned by Judith Hensley. I found Judith rearranging a display of spring scarves, their pastel colors perfectly complementing the new collection of hats perched on nearby pedestals.

"Good morning, Amanda." Judith tucked a stray silk scarf into place. "Listen, I've been meaning to tell you how pleased I am that you've joined the choir." Her expression sobered. "This current unpleasantness notwithstanding, of course. We need a strong alto like you."

"Let's hope the rest of the choir agrees." I ran my fingers over a lovely white wool coat with military-inspired brass buttons. It was cute as could be, but thoroughly impractical for the unpaved streets of Timber Coulee, which exploded into mud and dust the moment they weren't covered in snow.

Judith laughed, the sound brightening the quiet shop. I wandered toward a display of patriotic pins. Small enameled flags and red, white, and blue ribbons were arranged artfully on dark blue velvet. "These pins are lovely. New stock?"

"Just arrived last week. One dollar each, with fifty cents going to the Red Cross." Judith adjusted a slightly crooked pin. "They're selling faster than I can order them. Everyone wants to show their support these days."

"I'll take one." I opened my handbag and took out a dollar bill. "You know, Judith, I've been wondering about something."

"Oh?" She took the money and wrapped a flag pin in tissue paper.

"Have you noticed anything about how Molly's been treated since . . . what happened?"

Judith's hands paused mid-fold. "You mean people suspecting her? That's nonsense. Anyone who knows Molly knows she couldn't hurt a fly."

"But not everyone knows her well," I countered. "She hasn't lived here that long."

"Well, I've made it my business to tell anyone who'll listen that your niece is above suspicion." Her statement confirmed my suspicion that tongues were wagging. She handed me the wrapped pin with an emphatic nod. "Sheriff Holcomb will sort it all out, you mark my words."

"Speaking of sorting things out." I started to slip the pin into my handbag, then changed my mind, unfolded the tissue paper, and pinned the flag to my cardigan. "Have you any thoughts about . . . who might have wanted to harm Mary Alice?"

Judith glanced toward the front windows, then moved closer, lowering her voice. "Between us? Beatrice Fairmont had more reason than most."

"Because of her jealousy over the solo?"

"That, and because Mary Alice had been making comments about Henry's service." Judith's lips thinned. "Implying that driving an ambulance wasn't real service, that sort of thing. Beatrice was livid, understandably."

"That seems a bit extreme as a motive for murder." Though Mary Alice's cutting remarks about Clarence's military band service had rankled Molly.

"Perhaps. But there's another possibility." Judith leaned in closer. "Mary Alice was treasurer for Ladies' Aid, you know. The president, Mrs. Jenkins, told me there'd been some . . . tension over how Mary Alice managed the funds."

"Tension?"

"Apparently, Mary Alice kept a very tight rein on the purse strings. Questioned every expense, required receipts for the smallest purchases." Judith straightened a display of gloves. "Pearl Pritchard. You know her? Used to own the millinery shop on Cedar Street before she retired. Anyway, she practically had a conniption when Mary Alice demanded detailed accounting for war relief donations."

"Why would Mary Alice do that?"

"Who knows? She was always a stickler for rules. Mrs. Jenkins told me Pearl accused Mary Alice of implying she'd misused funds, right in the middle of a meeting!" Judith shook her head. "Pearl stormed out, saying she wouldn't be insulted like that."

"When was this?"

"Just a week or so ago, I believe." Judith pursed her lips thoughtfully. "Though I don't suppose Pearl would resort to murder over it."

"I wouldn't think so, but . . ." I hesitated. "Has anyone else outside the choir had troubles with Mary Alice? Someone we might not have thought about?"

Judith considered this. "Well, she did have that dispute with Mr. Tate at the bank. Something about rejecting a loan application for her nephew. But that was months ago." She straightened a hat on a nearby stand. "I suppose we've all had our moments with Mary Alice. She wasn't the easiest person to get along with."

That was putting it mildly. "It's unsettling to think someone among us might be capable of . . ." I couldn't finish the sentence.

"I know." Judith squeezed my arm. "At least we have the upcoming concert to distract us. Thank heaven Eleanor Crawford stepped in when she did."

"Speaking of Eleanor Crawford," I seized the opportunity to find out more about the newcomer, "she seems to be fitting in remarkably well for someone who's only been in town a short while."

Judith's face lit up. "She is an absolute treasure, isn't she? Such a refreshing presence, especially with everything that's happened. Having someone new in town with no connection to Mary Alice—it's a relief, isn't it?"

I studied a display of hatpins, trying to picture myself with a new friend, someone to confide in, someone who hadn't known Sarah, someone with no expectations or history in Timber Coulee. It was an appealing thought.

"She certainly has a gift for putting people at ease," I agreed. "She seemed so friendly, and I realized I don't know much about her, beyond what little you shared at rehearsal. How did you two meet?"

"Oh, it was the most fortuitous thing." Judith moved to the counter to jot something on a notepad. "She came into the shop, oh, around Eastertime, I think."

"That recently? I would have thought she'd been here longer, the way she's integrated into town life."

"That's Eleanor for you—never meets a stranger, as she says." Judith's pen moved across the page as she spoke. "She introduced herself as a writer for some women's magazine—*Angel of the Hearth*, I believe. Said she was working on an article about how women across the Western states are contributing to the war effort."

"How interesting that she's a magazine writer. Was she interviewing many people in town?"

"I'm not certain, though she seemed particularly interested in my perspective as a business owner." Pride crept into Judith's voice. "She asked the most thoughtful questions about how the war has affected women's fashion—how we're using narrower skirts to conserve fabric, simpler hat designs, and of course, all these military-inspired details." She gestured toward a mannequin sporting a white dress with a jaunty sailor collar.

"She certainly seems thorough in her research."

"Oh my, yes!" Judith closed her order book with a smile. "And she was so complimentary—said my window displays could rival those in any big city. Can you imagine?"

I could picture Eleanor's enthusiastic praise delivered in that warm drawl. "That sounds like her."

"You know," Judith lowered her voice slightly as if sharing a confidence, "she also mentioned she was looking to purchase some new clothes. Said she's just passed the one-year mark of her widowhood and is finally ready to set aside her mourning attire."

I calculated the timing. "So her husband would have died around April or May of last year?"

"Yes, very early in America's involvement in the war." Judith moved to straighten a lace collar on a nearby blouse. "Apparently they're quite strict about mourning periods in the South. She said proper Southern ladies observe six months in black, followed by six more months in lighter but still subdued colors like gray and navy, before transitioning to brighter colors."

"I thought those strict rules about mourning went out of fashion with the hoop skirt."

"So did I. But Eleanor explained it all. Said her Walter never did like dark colors on her anyway, and would have hated seeing her in black for so long." Judith sighed with sympathy. "The poor dear. He didn't even die in battle—caught some terrible virus that spread through the training camp. She said half his unit was lost before they ever reached France."

My heart ached for Eleanor. To lose her husband not to enemy fire but to illness seemed somehow more tragic—a pointless waste that couldn't even be draped in the glory of sacrifice for country.

"Did she purchase anything?" I asked.

"Not that day. Said she wasn't quite ready emotionally, though the calendar said she could." Judith's expression turned thoughtful. "I found that rather touching, don't you? Following the proper mourning period out of respect, but still feeling the loss too keenly to rush into bright colors."

"Very touching." I experienced a renewed surge of sympathy for Eleanor. My own grief for Sarah had been intense, but at least I hadn't been expected to mark it with a year of somber clothing. "Did she mention when she might return to shop?"

"She promised to come back soon. I've set aside a few pieces I think would suit her—nothing too bold, just softer colors to ease the transition." Judith's eyes brightened with professional enthusiasm. "With her coloring, she'll look stunning in deep blue or forest green.

"After we finished discussing fashion, she asked about meeting other ladies in town. Said she didn't know a soul here and was staying at the Timber Coulee Hotel while working on her article." Judith moved from behind the counter to adjust a sleeve on a blouse display. "I mentioned the Ladies' Aid Society, of course, and the Red Cross volunteers. Then I thought of the Meadowlarks, and I asked her if she liked music."

"And she just happened to play piano?" How fortunate that was for all of us.

"Isn't that providential?" Judith clapped her hands. "She laughed in that delightful way of hers and admitted she can't carry a tune in a bucket, but that she's played piano since she was 'knee-high to a grasshopper,' as she put it."

"A wonderful stroke of luck for the choir."

"Divine timing, I'd call it," Judith said. "And then, poor Mildred got that telegram about some situation in her family." She clucked her tongue. "I immediately thought of Eleanor, and it just came to me—why not ask her to fill in? The choir couldn't very well practice without accompaniment."

"How fortunate that she was willing." How nice it was to have someone like Eleanor who hadn't been tangled in Mary Alice's web of antagonism.

"Oh, she was more than willing—she was positively thrilled at the chance to be useful, as she put it. And it will give her an opportunity to get to know some other ladies, like you." Judith gave me a fond smile. "You know, I feel like I've known her forever, though it's been just a short while. She has that quality about her."

"She does indeed." I fingered the price tag on a navy-blue hat, considering. "Has she mentioned how long she'll be staying in Timber Coulee?"

"Not specifically, though she did say something about her article deadline being flexible." Judith angled the flag-pin display toward the window so the brightly colored metal would catch more light. "Between you and me, I think she might be looking to put down roots. She's asked about real estate in town—nothing specific, just wondering about property values and such."

"Really?" This caught my attention. A small flutter of excitement rose in my chest at the thought of having a new friend permanently in town. "I believe Ernie Wendell's old house is still vacant. It's small, but a nice size for a single person."

"Is it? Well, I'll mention it to her, if I remember."

"I'll talk to her about it. We're meeting for tea later today."

"Oh, are you?" Judith beamed. "I'm glad. I can picture you two becoming fast friends."

Secretly, I hoped so. Other than young Molly, I hadn't had a truly close friend since Sarah—someone closer to my own age, who shared my love of music and books and my sometimes quirky outlook on life. "It would be nice if she'd move here to town."

"Wouldn't it, though? She mentioned being able to do her writing job from just about anywhere. We could certainly use someone with her talents and spirit." Judith sighed with contentment. "And such a lovely pianist. Poor Mildred tries her best, bless her heart, but Eleanor has a real gift."

"Have you heard from Mildred?" I chose my words carefully, so as not to betray the sheriff's suspicions. "How is her family member doing?"

A shadow crossed Judith's face. "No, I haven't. But she's only been gone a few days. I do hope everything's all right."

The shop door opened, and a woman walked in with her daughter in tow. Judith immediately switched into her shopkeeper persona, greeting them warmly.

"I must be off." I picked up my handbag. "Molly will be wondering where I am."

"Of course, dear." Judith patted my forearm as I passed. "Oh, and Amanda? Do tell Eleanor I said hello. And if you get a chance, ask her about her article. I'd love to know when it might be published."

"I certainly will."

Outside, the May morning had turned balmy. I unbuttoned my cardigan, mulling over what I'd learned. Beatrice had a clear motive, according to Judith. And this

Pearl Pritchard from the Ladies' Aid Society seemed worth looking into as well. I'd have to ask around about her.

But what lifted my spirits most was the prospect of tea with Eleanor later. There was something refreshing about spending time with someone who had no connection to Mary Alice or the snarled web of small-town relationships. Someone new, with a fresh perspective. Someone who might become a friend.

As I walked toward Mountain Melodies, I found myself genuinely smiling for the first time in days.

Chapter Nine

The Hummingbird Tearoom had opened just a month earlier in what used to be a men's haberdashery on Elm Street. With its lace curtains, delicate china, and the scent of fresh-baked scones wafting through the air, it provided a much-needed refuge from the tensions that had enveloped Timber Coulee since Mary Alice's murder. Had it only been five days? It seemed like so much longer.

I arrived a few minutes early and selected a table by the window, where I could see townspeople going about their business, their faces still carrying the strain of recent events. Sheriff Holcomb's warning to exercise caution had spread throughout the town like wildfire, turning our usually friendly community suspicious and wary.

The door opened and Eleanor appeared. I recognized the American flag pinned to her lapel—an exact match to mine. Her cheeks were flushed from the warm spring air, giving her an almost girlish appearance. As she made her way to my table, several patrons turned to watch her with the undisguised curiosity that small towns reserve for newcomers.

"Oh, my goodness, I hope I haven't kept you waitin', sugar." Her dark eyes twinkled with genuine warmth.

"Not at all. I was enjoying the quiet."

Eleanor glanced around with a delighted air. "What an absolute treasure of a place! Reminds me of my granny's parlor back in Georgia. So different from those stuffy tearooms in Portland."

I was about to respond when a slender young girl approached our table. Viola Thornton's dark hair was neatly pinned back in a style too severe for her sixteen years, though tendrils had escaped to frame her pale face. She wore a simple blue dress with a crisp white apron tied at her waist.

"Good afternoon, Miss Parrish," she murmured, eyes downcast.

"Viola, I didn't know you were working here." I smiled warmly at the girl, hoping to draw her out of her shell.

She glanced briefly toward the kitchen. "Mrs. Talbott hired me last week. After school and Saturdays. She said she needed more help since she and Mr. Talbott have been working with the Red Cross, and—" Her fingers twisted nervously in her apron. "The extra money is . . . helpful."

I understood her meaning, mindful of what Molly had confided to me about her brother Edward's situation. The Thornton family was likely struggling. Rather than embarrass her by acknowledging this, I turned to make introductions.

"Viola, this is Eleanor Crawford, our new choir accompanist. Eleanor, Viola Thornton sings in the soprano section with Molly."

"Well, aren't you just the prettiest little songbird!" Eleanor's smile broadened, Southern charm on full display. "It's a pleasure to meet you, sweetheart. I noticed your lovely voice at rehearsal."

Viola's cheeks colored slightly at the compliment. "Thank you, Mrs. Crawford."

"Oh, honey, call me Eleanor. Everyone does." Eleanor leaned forward conspiratorially. "Mrs. Crawford makes me feel older than Methuselah."

A hint of a smile touched Viola's lips before disappearing just as quickly. "May I take your order, or would you like to see a menu first?"

"What do you recommend, darlin'?" Eleanor asked.

"The orange spice tea is our special today." Viola's gaze flicked toward the kitchen, where Mrs. Talbott was watching with an eagle eye. "And the scones are fresh from the oven."

"That sounds absolutely divine," Eleanor exclaimed. "Don't you think so, Amanda?"

I nodded. "Two pots of orange spice and a plate of scones, please, Viola."

"Such a sweet girl," Eleanor commented after Viola disappeared into the kitchen. "Isn't that the sister of the soldier with the gamblin' problem?"

I nearly choked. "I'm sorry?"

Eleanor's eyes widened slightly. "Oh dear, perhaps I've misspoken. I thought everyone knew. There was talk at the post office yesterday about the Thornton boy gettin' himself into debt troubles overseas."

"How on earth did you hear about that?"

Eleanor blinked, her hand fluttering to her throat. "Why, I just overheard some ladies talkin', sugar. You know how small towns are—everyone seems to know everyone else's business." She leaned forward, lowering her voice. "I certainly didn't mean to gossip. It's just that the poor family seemed distressed, and I thought perhaps the choir ladies might organize some kind of help."

I pressed my lips together, trying to quell my irritation. Edward Thornton's gambling had indeed been the subject of whispers around town, but the Thorntons had worked hard to keep the matter private. To hear a newcomer so casually referencing their troubles stirred a protective instinct in me.

"I prefer not to discuss other people's private matters." The comment came out sounding starchier than I'd intended. "Especially when they involve families with loved ones overseas."

Eleanor's face fell. "Oh, my stars, I've upset you. I'm so terribly sorry, Amanda." She reached across to touch my hand. "You're absolutely right to scold me. My granny would've taken a switch to my legs for that kind of loose talk. Please forgive me."

Her contrition seemed genuine, and my irritation ebbed. "It's all right. I just . . . Timber Coulee has its share of gossips, but I try not to be one of them."

"And you're right as rain about that." Eleanor's expression was earnest. "I promise to be more mindful. The last thing I want is to add to anyone's burdens during these difficult times."

To change the subject I asked, "You say you came here from Portland?" Any topic would suffice, as long as it had nothing to do with murder or war or other people's personal business.

"Bless your heart, no. I spent some time there after . . ." She paused, a cloud passing over her expression. "After my Walter passed. But I grew up in Georgia, sweet tea and magnolias and all."

Curiosity got the better of me. "If you don't mind my asking, how did you end up in Timber Coulee? It's not exactly on the way to anywhere."

"Isn't that the truth!" She laughed, the sound as lyrical as her piano playing. "But sometimes the best places aren't on anybody's map. And I've seen a lot of 'em. As Judith told y'all at choir practice, I'm a travelin' correspondent for *Angel of the Hearth* magazine. I'm doin' a feature on how women in the West are copin' during wartime—their strength, their sacrifices, their everyday courage."

"That sounds fascinating." I'd never heard of *Angel of the Hearth*, but then I seldom had time to read anything beyond a music-industry journal and my beloved detective novels.

"Oh, it is! These stories need tellin', and I'm honored to be the one to do it." Her eyes shone with genuine passion. "I met your lovely Judith while interviewin' her at her dress shop—how she's adaptin' to fabric rationin' and such. Somehow we got to talkin' about music, and I mentioned I played piano since I was a tiny little thing."

Her smile deepened, revealing dimples. "Next thing I know, she's tellin' me about poor Miss Abernathy bein' called away so sudden-like for her family emergency, and how the choir was in a pickle without an accompanist. It felt like divine timin', truly it did. That's what Judith called it—divine timin'."

"So you stepped in." I warmed even more to this generous woman.

"How could I resist? We musicians have to stick together, especially durin' these troubled times." She tilted her head like a curious wren. "Now tell me all about yourself, Amanda. I feel like we're kindred spirits, if you don't mind my sayin' so. Two Debussy lovers in this lovely little town."

"It was completely unplanned. I was on a train from Chicago to Seattle twelve years ago when we got stranded here in a terrible blizzard."

"My stars! Like somethin' from a novel!"

"It felt that way," I agreed. "I was supposed to be taking a position teaching music at a school in Washington, but during several days of waiting for the tracks to clear, I fell in love with this town."

"I can certainly see why."

"The local general store had a small section for sheet music, and the owner mentioned how folks were always asking for more variety, and for musical instruments and lessons for the children. There was no music shop within fifty miles." The memory of that moment of inspiration warmed my heart. "I saw my opportunity and seized it.

The man introduced me to a Scotsman, a talented violinist named Callan MacTavish, who also had ideas about opening a music shop. Long story short, we agreed to be business partners, and by the time the tracks were cleared, we'd already inquired about renting a building. I telegraphed my regrets to the school in Seattle and never looked back."

"What a delightful story! Talk about followin' your heart." Eleanor's eyes sparkled. "Is Mr. MacTavish still your partner?"

"*Business* partner," I clarified firmly. "He's happily married to Rose, and they have a young son, Emil. But when the war broke out in Europe, he felt a strong pull of duty to join the British military to defend his homeland. So he left, and I've been running the shop alone since then. Except for my niece, Molly Mulroney. You may have met her at the Meadowlarks rehearsal."

"Did she accompany you from Chicago?"

"No, she came out for a visit and decided to stay. She'd been studying violin at the conservatory in Chicago, but her heart wasn't in it. She was doing it mostly to please her parents—my sister and her husband." Too late, I closed my lips. It wasn't my place to share Molly's business with this relative stranger.

Eleanor seemed to sense my reticence. "Family can be as tangled as a ball of yarn after a kitten's had at it, can't it? No need to explain, sugar. The important thing is she's here now, and you have each other."

"Yes, exactly." Relieved at her understanding, I brought the conversation back to her situation. "It can't be easy, joining a community at such a difficult time as this."

"Well now, I won't pretend it's been a cakewalk." Her expression softened. "But my granny always said trouble shared is trouble halved. Music has a way of bringin' folks together when nothin' else can. It speaks all the words our hearts can't find."

I found myself studying Eleanor's animated face—the graceful arch of her eyebrows, the slight crease at the corners of her eyes suggesting frequent smiles, the warmth that seemed to radiate from her very being.

"You mentioned your husband," I said finally. "I'm sorry for your loss."

"Thank you, darlin'." She dropped her gaze to the gingham tablecloth and spoke barely above a whisper. Her fingers reached out to briefly squeeze mine, a gesture of shared understanding. "Walter died at Verdun."

"How terrible." But even as I expressed sympathy, a couple of details nagged at my brain. Judith had said he'd died of a virus, not in battle. And that he'd died a year ago, in spring, yet the Battle of Verdun had taken place in the fall.

Eleanor was saying something about troubles being meant to strengthen us.

"Please excuse me—Judith told me he'd died of a virus." I hoped my question wasn't rude, but I had to know.

Her eyes tightened almost imperceptibly. "Yes. That's right. He caught a virus while workin' in Verdun on some engineerin' project."

My mind cleared. "Oh, you mean the *town* of Verdun. Not the battle." That made perfect sense.

"Yes, of course," she said. "I should have been more specific."

My face heated. After all my lofty comments about being above gossip, here I was admitting I'd been discussing her situation with Judith. But if Eleanor minded, she didn't let on.

"We had no children, which was a blessin' in its way." Her voice wavered slightly, though her smile remained brave. "No little ones left behind. But I do so love children—one of the reasons I'm tickled pink to hear you have a niece."

"Oh, Molly's not a child anymore. The fact of which I have to continually remind myself."

The tearoom felt cozy, warmed by Eleanor's easy charm. My old friend Sarah's face flashed in my mind—not as I'd last seen her, gray and still in her coffin, but laughing as she and James danced at the town's Founder's Day celebration the summer before her illness.

Viola returned with our tea and a plate of scones, mercifully breaking the moment. "Fresh from the oven," she announced. "And clotted cream from the Hendersons' dairy."

"My goodness, these look divine!" Eleanor exclaimed. "You know, food is truly love made visible. My granny used to say that." She prepared her tea with delicate movements, somehow managing to seem both graceful and homey at once. She looked at me over her teacup. "And you? Are you married?"

"No," I admitted. "Though my niece has become something like a daughter to me."

"What a blessin' for both of you!" Eleanor's face lit up. "There's nothin' like family. Even chosen family, which can be the sweetest kind. She's lucky to have an aunt like you, and I bet you're just as lucky to have her bright spirit around."

"It is wonderful." Eleanor's enthusiasm was contagious. "She helps me in the shop, and she's quite a talented violinist herself. I do wish she'd completed her studies at the conservatory, but maybe she'll go back at some point."

"And she has a young man fightin' overseas, I understand?" Eleanor's face softened with genuine concern.

"Yes, Clarence Butterworth. They met the summer before last at the local music camp. He's serving with the 91st
Infantry Division Band." I couldn't keep a note of pride
from my voice. "He's a trumpeter—first chair. His letters
say the soldiers cherish the music. A bit of home in that
hellish place."

"How brave they both are." Eleanor placed a hand over
her heart. "She waitin' faithfully, he usin' his beautiful gift
to lift spirits in such darkness. Music sustains the soul
when nothin' else can, doesn't it?" She broke a scone in
half, releasing a wisp of steam. "Are there many other families in Timber Coulee with loved ones at the front? I'd love
to help organize care packages or somethin', if I could be
of service."

"More than our fair share, I'm afraid. Timber Coulee
has always been patriotic to a fault." The gold stars in windows throughout town attested to that, each representing
a son, brother, or husband who wouldn't return.

"The waitin' must be unbearable for these families.
Wonderin' each day if news will come. I remember those
feelin's all too well." She dabbed at the corner of her eye
with a lace handkerchief.

"It is difficult," I agreed. "The Red Cross has been organizing support groups for military families. They meet in
the church basement on Wednesday evenings."

"Do they help with practical matters too? Allotments and such? So many women are just overwhelmed by paperwork when their men are away. I'd be happy to volunteer my time. After Walter passed, I learned more than I ever wanted to about military paperwork, and if I could spare another woman even a little of that confusion, well, I'd consider that a real blessin'."

"I believe they do." I spread a bit of clotted cream on my scone. "Mrs. Jenkins from the Ladies' Aid Society has been helping women navigate the paperwork. It can be quite confusing, especially for those who've never managed household finances before."

"Indeed it can be, poor souls." Eleanor's gaze drifted to the window, where Sheriff Holcomb was crossing the street. His eyes flicked to the tearoom and met mine briefly. He touched the brim of his hat, then moved on. "My goodness, your sheriff is certainly handsome. And dedicated to his work, I can tell."

"James is a most capable lawman." I hoped the sudden warmth in my cheeks wasn't visible. "The town is fortunate to have him."

"You know him well?" Her expression was knowing but kind, without a hint of teasing.

"We've known each other a long time." I hesitated, uncertain how much to share. "His late wife, Sarah, was one of my dearest friends."

Understanding dawned in Eleanor's eyes. "Grief has its own timetable, doesn't it? And shared memories can be both a comfort and a burden."

I wasn't sure whether to be discomfited or relieved by her perception. "We're managing. This current murder investigation has complicated things, of course."

"I can only imagine." Eleanor reached across to pat my hand. "Trust is so fragile after violence touches a community. But you know what my granny always said? 'Even the darkest night will end and the sun will rise.' This town will heal, sugar. Good people always find their way back to each other."

"Were you an army wife for long?" Anything to steer the conversation away from James.

"Five years." Her eyes held a wistfulness that seemed genuine. "We moved more often than a tumbleweed in a tornado—San Francisco, Denver, Fort Lewis near Tacoma. Walter's engineerin' skills were in high demand."

"That must have been difficult, never putting down roots."

"It taught me to bloom where I'm planted," she said with a lilting laugh. "Though I admit I've been longin' for a smaller community. Somewhere to make real connections. Somewhere to belong."

"Well, Timber Coulee could certainly use more talented musicians. I know of a little house for sale that would be perfect for you." I avoided mentioning that the house in question had been the scene of yet another murder, lest she think Timber Coulee was a hotbed of homicide.

She gave me an odd look. "It's a little premature for me to start lookin' at houses."

"Of course," I murmured, tempering my enthusiasm. Just because I was desperate for a new friend didn't mean she was.

"Tell me more about your music shop." Her eyes lit with interest. "I've been meanin' to look for some new Victrola records. I have a weakness for ragtime that borders on sinful. And I'll bring you some of my granny's famous pecan cookies."

As I described Mountain Melodies, its history and the joy it had brought me over the years, some of the tension that had gripped me since Mary Alice's death began to ease. Eleanor listened attentively, asking thoughtful questions and exclaiming with genuine delight over details that most people would find mundane.

As we prepared to leave, she gently touched my hand. "Thank you for this, Amanda. You've been a ray of sunshine in what's been a mighty gloomy time. It's not easy makin' friends in a new place, especially under such circumstances."

"I've enjoyed it too." It was true. Despite the shadow of recent events, despite the grief and fear that had permeated every conversation in the past week, I'd found genuine pleasure in Eleanor's company.

As we walked to the door, Viola came to collect our teacups, her expression once again solemn. Eleanor paused to leave a generous tip under her saucer, carefully folding the bills so they wouldn't be immediately visible to other patrons.

"It was lovely meetin' you, Viola," she called softly. "I hope to see you at our next rehearsal."

Viola nodded, a fleeting smile crossing her face before she returned to her work.

Eleanor and I parted at the corner. As I waved good-bye, my heart lifted with the joy that comes from having, at last, found a kindred spirit.

Chapter Ten

The following Monday, a week after the murder, I found Molly and Viola in the room at the rear of the shop, which had mercifully transformed from a horrific crime scene back into an ordinary storage and rehearsal space. Molly stood behind Viola, gently correcting the younger woman's hold on the bow.

"That's it," Molly encouraged as Viola drew the bow across the strings, producing a tremulous but sweet note. "Now try the whole phrase."

I waited until they finished before entering. Viola's face, previously tense with concentration, broke into a smile at the sight of me.

"Miss Parrish! Molly's been teaching me 'Rock of Ages.' Would you like to hear?"

"I'd love to." I leaned against the doorframe.

Viola's performance was hesitant but earnest, and I applauded heartily when she finished. Her cheeks flushed with pleasure at the praise—perhaps the first real happiness I'd seen on her face since Mary Alice's murder.

"You have a natural ear," I told her. "Have you played before?"

"Father bought me a violin for my sixteenth birthday," she admitted. "But with the war and Edward's enlistment, there hasn't been money for lessons."

Molly adjusted the instrument's tuning. "I've told Viola she's welcome to practice here anytime. The violin was just gathering dust anyway."

I nodded my approval, wondering if Molly's generosity stemmed partly from concern over the Thorntons' financial situation. Before I could pursue the thought, Moxie darted between my ankles with an indignant meow. The shop bell jingled a moment later.

"Hello?" called a lilting Southern voice. "Anybody home?"

"We're in the back," I called.

Eleanor appeared in the doorway, carrying a small wicker basket covered with a checkered cloth.

"I hope I'm not interruptin'," she said with a honeyed smile. "But I promised those pecan cookies, and my granny always said a promise delayed is a promise betrayed."

"How thoughtful of you." The delicious aroma of butter, sugar, and pecans wafted through the room as she uncovered the basket. "But how did you manage to bake cookies in a hotel room?"

"Oh, goodness, sugar." She laughed. "That would have been quite a feat, wouldn't it? No, I gave my recipe to Mrs. Wasserman and paid her to bake them for me. So you really have her to thank, more than me. I'm just passin' them on."

On the floor beside me, Moxie's ears had flattened against his head the moment Eleanor entered the room. Now his fur bristled along his spine, and he let out a low, unmistakable growl.

"Oh, my," Eleanor took a step back. "Someone doesn't seem pleased to see me—ah . . . ah . . . ACHOO!" She fumbled for a handkerchief. "Goodness gracious, excuse me! I'm afraid I've always had a terrible reaction to cats." She gave a dainty dab to her nose.

"Moxie, behave yourself," I scolded. The cat wrapped himself around my ankles. "I'm so sorry. He's usually quite sociable with visitors."

"It's the allergies," Eleanor managed between sniffles. "Animals can sense these things. I start sneezin', and they think I'm hissin' at 'em." She attempted a light laugh that dissolved into another sneeze.

I scooped up the stiff, resistant feline. "I'll put him out-side." Moxie struggled in my arms, his eyes never leaving

Eleanor, a low growl rumbling in his chest as I carried him away.

"You're too kind." Eleanor's watery eyes somehow still managed to sparkle as she composed herself. Her gaze fell on Viola. "Miss Thornton, isn't it? How lovely to see you again, sugar! My, you play beautifully."

Viola's face lit up at the compliment. "Thank you, Mrs. Crawford. I mean, Eleanor. I'm just a beginner, really."

"Nonsense!" Eleanor waved away her modesty. "I can always recognize natural talent. My father taught music at the Atlanta Conservatory for thirty years." She extended the basket toward Viola. "Cookie, darlin'? Fresh from the oven this mornin'. Mrs. Wasserman's oven, that is."

"Thank you." Viola selected a cookie with obvious delight. Her earlier reticence seemed to have melted away completely in the warmth of Eleanor's attention.

"Would you like one, too?" Eleanor extended the basket to Molly, who took one.

"Thanks, Mrs. Crawford."

"It's Eleanor, please." She turned back to Viola. "I spoke with your mother after church last Sunday. Such a gracious lady. She mentioned you might be interested in joinin' the church junior choir as well?"

"I'd like to," Viola admitted. "But Mother worries about the extra time away from home, especially with all the chores since Edward left."

Eleanor's expression softened with perfect sympathy. "Of course, family must come first. But perhaps we could work somethin' out? I'd be happy to help your mother with some of those chores if it would allow you to pursue your musical gifts."

Viola's eyes widened. "That's . . . that's very kind of you."

"Not at all! What are neighbors for, if not to help each other durin' difficult times?" Eleanor placed the basket on a nearby shelf. "Now, don't let me interrupt your lesson. In fact, I'd love to stay and listen, if that's all right with everyone?"

Molly nodded, though I detected a hint of reservation in her expression. "We were just about to try the second stanza."

As Viola resumed her position and raised the violin, I excused myself to serve a customer at the front counter. By the time I returned, Viola was playing with noticeably more confidence while Eleanor offered enthusiastic encouragement.

"Beautiful, just beautiful!" she exclaimed when Viola finished. "With a little more practice, you could easily perform that at the Sunday service."

"Do you really think so?" Viola's face flushed with pleasure.

"I know talent when I hear it, sugar," Eleanor assured her. She glanced at the clock on the wall. "Goodness me, is that the time? I must be off."

"I should be heading home too." Viola carefully returned the violin to its case. "Mother will be wondering where I am."

"Will you be back tonight for choir rehearsal?" I asked.

"I'm not certain. I'll try. It'll depend on the situation at home."

"Why don't I walk with you, darlin'?" Eleanor suggested. "It's on my way to the hotel, and I'd love to hear more about your musical aspirations."

"That would be lovely," Viola agreed with a smile that transformed her usually solemn face.

I felt a small surge of satisfaction seeing the girl so animated. Eleanor's arrival in town seemed to be a blessing in many ways, bringing warmth and encouragement where it was sorely needed.

As Viola and Eleanor gathered their things, the door opened again. I turned and found James standing near the counter, hat in hand, while Eleanor and Viola emerged from the practice room, Eleanor carrying the basket of cookies. The moment she spotted him, her entire demeanor transformed.

"Why, Sheriff Holcomb," she purred, gliding toward him. "What a pleasant surprise! I was just thinkin' about our law enforcement hero."

James's posture stiffened visibly. "Mrs. Crawford." He gave a curt nod. "Good afternoon. I trust your article is coming along."

"Research never ends," she replied, stepping closer than propriety typically allowed. "Though I must say, if all my interviews were with gentlemen as distinguished as yourself, I'd never want to finish." She held forth the basket. "Cookie?"

A flush crept up James's neck as he took a subtle step back. "No, thank you. I'm here on official business, ma'am."

"Official business sounds so . . . serious." Eleanor's eyelashes fluttered. "Perhaps you could explain it to me sometime? Over supper, maybe?"

An unexpected pang of irritation plucked my heartstrings at her forward behavior. James and I weren't courting—we'd never acknowledged the unspoken tension between us—but Eleanor's blatant flirtation still rankled.

"Miss Parrish," James turned to me with obvious relief, "might I have a word about your recent roof repairs? The station roof has a leak, and I'd like to know what you thought of Drummond's work."

It was a transparent excuse, but I played along. "Of course. We can discuss it in the back room. I'll show you what he fixed."

Eleanor watched us with an odd intensity that made me slightly uncomfortable. "Come along, Viola," she said finally. "We should let the sheriff attend to his official business. So much to do, so little time." She set the basket with the remaining cookies on the counter. "You can return the basket later, sugar." She turned to James with one last lingering glance. "Sheriff, I do hope our paths cross again soon."

As she brushed past him toward the door, she let out another delicate sneeze. James stepped aside quickly, visibly awkward with her proximity.

"Toodle-oo," Eleanor called. The girl followed, her step lighter than I'd seen in weeks, offering a small wave to Molly as she left.

When the door finally closed behind them, James exhaled audibly. "I appreciate your chance to discuss . . . roof repairs, Miss Parrish."

"Always happy to discuss roof repairs," I replied. "What's really on your mind, James?"

He glanced toward the storeroom where Molly was banging things around, then lowered his voice. "I wanted to update you on the investigation. As a friend."

My heart quickened. "Have you found something new?"

"We've been looking into Beatrice Fairmont's background." His expression was unreadable. "She has . . . connections that are concerning."

"Connections?" I frowned. "You can't possibly think Beatrice had anything to do with Mary Alice's death."

"I'm following every lead." He spoke slowly, carefully. "Mary Alice had been asking questions about certain people in town, including Mrs. Fairmont's correspondence with her son's commanding officer."

"How could she possibly know about that?"

"That's what we're trying to determine." James ran a hand through his hair, a gesture I recognized as one of frustration. "There's also the matter of the knitting needles found with the body. They match the set Beatrice was using during rehearsal."

"Half the women in the choir use identical needles," I pointed out. "They were bought in bulk for the soldiers' sock project."

James nodded. "I'm aware. Which is why we haven't ruled out . . . other possibilities." His gaze flickered briefly toward the storeroom.

I stiffened. "Molly had nothing to do with this."

"I know you believe that," he said gently, "and I hope you're right. But I have to follow the evidence wherever it leads." His expression softened slightly. "For what it's worth, I think there's more to this case than a simple argument that got out of hand."

"What do you mean?"

"Mary Alice seems to have been collecting information on several people in town, particularly those with family members serving overseas. We're still trying to understand why."

"You think that might be connected to her death?"

"It's possible." James placed his hat back on his head. "Amanda . . . do be careful whom you trust. This town isn't as simple as it once was."

"The war has changed everything," I murmured.

"Not everything." His eyes met mine briefly, and I caught a glimpse of the man behind the sheriff's badge—the man who had once been my friend, who might have been more if circumstances had been different. "I should go. Deputy Peterson is interviewing Mrs. Fairmont again this afternoon."

As he turned to leave, I found myself saying, "James, about Eleanor Crawford . . ."

He paused. "What about her?"

It was a good question. Why *had* I brought her name up? I had no reason to suspect Eleanor of anything improper. She seemed to take a special interest in Viola, but I couldn't connect it to anything sinister. She'd been nothing but charming and friendly since her arrival, even if her attention to James was a bit forward.

"Nothing," I said finally, setting aside my vague and unsettled feeling. "It's just . . . she seems quite taken with you."

A grimace crossed his face. "So I've noticed. Good day, Miss Parrish."

As he left, Molly watched us from the doorway to the storeroom, her expression troubled.

"Does Sheriff Holcomb still think I killed her?" Her fingers twisted the edge of her work smock, a nervous habit she'd had since childhood.

"No," I answered quickly—perhaps too quickly. "He's focused on Beatrice Fairmont. As well as Mildred Abernathy, I assume."

"But I'm not completely eliminated from his list, am I?" Her eyes searched my face for reassurance I wasn't sure I could honestly give.

I sighed and crossed to the counter, absently picking up a dust cloth. "James has to follow the evidence, Molly. But we know you didn't do this."

"The knitting needles found with Mary Alice . . ."

"Were identical to needles half the women in town use," I finished firmly. "It proves nothing."

"But my yarn—"

"—could have been taken by anyone during rehearsal," I countered. "Especially since you left it here when you walked Viola home."

Molly leaned against the counter, worry clouding her features. "Did he say why he suspects Beatrice?"

"Apparently, Mary Alice had been asking questions about her. About her 'connections,' whatever that means."

"Mary Alice was always asking questions about everyone," Molly said. "She collected other people's secrets like some folks collect stamps."

I glanced at my niece. "You don't believe Beatrice did it, do you?"

"Do you?" she challenged.

We stood in silence for a moment, the late afternoon sunlight casting long shadows across the Victrola display.

"No," I admitted finally. "Beatrice has a sharp tongue, but she's not a killer."

"Mrs. Crawford seems to have taken a shine to Viola," Molly observed, changing the subject. "She was all compliments and encouragement during the lesson."

"It's nice to see Viola looking happier." I sampled one of Eleanor's cookies. It was delicious—buttery and rich with just the right amount of sweetness. "Eleanor seems to have a gift for bringing out the best in people."

"Hmm," was Molly's only response as she took a cookie for herself.

"You don't agree?"

Molly paused before responding. "It's not that. She's perfectly pleasant. It's just . . . everything about her seems so well calculated. The accent, the stories, the compliments."

"Some people are naturally charming," I said with a shrug. "Not everyone has your suspicion of strangers."

"It's served me well so far," Molly replied with a smile that fell short of genuine.

As I gathered up the remaining cookies to take home for later, I couldn't help but wonder if I was missing something about our new friend. But then, these were suspicious times, and no one had been left untouched by the shadow Mary Alice's murder had cast over our town.

Chapter Eleven

Mindful of what Judith had told me about Pearl Pritchard's altercation with Mary Alice over the Ladies' Aid Society's war relief fund, I decided to pay a visit to the society's president, Mrs. Jenkins, a fellow Meadowlark with whom I had a passing acquaintance. Without questioning her directly, I hoped to subtly get her take on what exactly had transpired between Pearl and Mary Alice, and whether the disagreement had been serious enough to lead to homicide.

Mrs. Jenkins lived in a modest white clapboard house near the library. I felt like an intruder as I balanced a stack of Victrola records in my arms and climbed the front steps.

Mrs. Jenkins greeted me at the door, her silver-framed spectacles perched on the end of her nose. "Amanda! What a lovely surprise."

"I found these while organizing the shop," I explained, offering the records. "Thought they might be useful for the young people's Fortnightly dances."

"How thoughtful." She ushered me inside. "We're just finishing our monthly accounts. It's been chaos since . . ." Her voice trailed off as she accepted the stack.

"Since Mary Alice," I finished for her.

"Yes." She lowered her voice. "Between us, I'm not sure how we'll manage. Mary Alice kept the books with such precision." She sighed. "Though her methods were sometimes a bit . . . forceful."

I followed Mrs. Jenkins into her dining room where, to my surprise, several society members huddled around a large table covered with ledgers and papers. The otherwise orderly space looked as though a cyclone had struck an accounting office. "Ladies, look what Amanda has brought us," Mrs. Jenkins announced.

A chorus of distracted thank-yous rose from the group. I recognized Beatrice Fairmont among them, her knitting needles clicking away despite the accounting crisis surrounding her.

I had expected to visit with Mrs. Jenkins alone. "I'd offer to help, but I can see you're all quite busy."

"It's these donation records." Honey Whitaker looked up from a leather-bound ledger. "Mary Alice had her own system, and none of us can make heads nor tails of it."

"She was very particular about the war relief funds," Mrs. Jenkins added. "Insisted on handling everything herself."

I moved closer to the table, curiosity piqued. "Were there many donations?"

"Oh, yes." Mrs. Jenkins nodded. "The town has been wonderfully generous. Everyone wants to support our boys overseas."

I glanced at the open ledger. Mary Alice's handwriting was as precise as her singing—perfect cursive rows with dates, names, and amounts. But something caught my eye: small pencil marks next to certain entries. Dots and question marks that seemed intentionally inconspicuous.

"She kept asking the most impertinent questions," Mrs. Jenkins confided as she adjusted her spectacles. "Wanting to know exactly who had access to the donations, demanding copies of bank receipts."

"Meticulous, in other words." I tried to keep my tone casual.

"It was quite vexing," Mrs. Jenkins agreed. "Though Pearl took the brunt of it, poor thing."

Bingo. "Pearl Pritchard?" I asked.

"Yes. Mary Alice practically accused her of mismanagement. Can you imagine? After twenty years of exemplary service." Mrs. Jenkins shook her head in disapproval. "Said she'd found discrepancies in the accounts."

I cleared my throat. "Someone told me their discussion got pretty heated."

"I'll say," Beatrice piped up from her seat in the corner. "I thought they'd come to blows, for sure."

"Really?" I could name several people who'd likely been tempted to wallop Mary Alice at one time or another, but no one who'd actually act on it. "Surely that's an exaggeration."

"Ask her yourself." Beatrice pointed with her knitting needle. "Here she comes now."

From the kitchen door emerged a tiny woman who looked ninety years old if she was a day, leaning on a cane. Hunched and frail, she peered up at me through thick spectacles and opened her lips in a toothless grin. "Hello, dear." Her voice creaked like a rusty hinge. "Have you brought the doughnuts?"

Before I could respond, Beatrice's foghorn voice blared, "THAT'S NOT THE DOUGHNUT GIRL, PEARL. IT'S AMANDA PARRISH."

"Eh? A donation from the parish?" Pearl looked confused. "Which parish—Catholic or Episcopal?"

Mentally I crossed Pearl Pritchard off my list of suspects. There was no way this feeble nonagenarian could have strangled Mary Alice, no matter how angry she'd been.

But Beatrice was another matter. As she wielded her knitting needles, I could see there was plenty of strength left in those beefy arms.

The doorbell rang, and Mrs. Jenkins excused herself. I lingered near the table, pretending to organize the record albums while straining to hear the conversation taking place at the far end.

". . . definitely missing," came a whispered voice. "The April deposits don't match what was collected."

"Could be a simple accounting error," another voice replied.

"Or perhaps Mary Alice was right all along."

I busied myself with the gramophone records as Honey Whitaker approached, her brow furrowed. "We're all so concerned about your niece. How is she holding up?"

"Fine, thanks," I said with forced cheer. "She's minding the shop, and she's started giving Viola Thornton violin lessons. The poor girl needed a distraction from her family troubles." Just as Honey needed a distraction from her nosy questions about Molly.

Honey's expression softened. "Yes, I heard about the Thornton boy. Such a shame. And now with this letter demanding money—"

I stared at her. "You know about that?"

"Small town," she replied with a slight shrug. "Mrs. Thornton confided in Mrs. Swanson, and, well . . ." She didn't need to finish the sentence. In Timber Coulee, confidences rarely stayed that way for long.

"Do you think it's legitimate?" I asked carefully. "The letter, I mean."

Honey shrugged. "I wouldn't know. But the Thorntons seem convinced. They're meeting with the bank tomorrow regarding a loan."

When Mrs. Jenkins returned, I made my excuses to leave, my mind racing with questions. Why had Mary Alice been scrutinizing the war relief donations? What discrepancies had she found? And was there any connection to the suspiciously timed letter to the Thorntons about their son's supposed gambling debts?

Chapter Twelve

Mildred's cottage sat back from the road, partially hidden by two tall white pines. Its blue shutters were fading, and the small garden showed signs of neglect—unusual for Mildred, who typically kept her flowers as well arranged as her piano scores.

I approached the front door with growing unease. What exactly did I expect to find? And was I crossing some line by investigating on my own? James would certainly think so.

The porch creaked beneath my feet as I gave a tentative knock. No answer came, as expected. After a moment's hesitation, I tried the door handle. Locked.

I peered through the lace-curtained window. The interior looked tidy but hastily abandoned—a teacup still sat on the side table, a book lay open on the sofa as if Mildred had just stepped away for a moment rather than embarking on a journey.

At the back of the house, the kitchen curtains were open. Inside, everything appeared normal, with dishes dried in the rack and a kettle on the stove. But there was something odd—a drawer left ajar, papers spilling out.

Looking around to ensure no neighbors were watching, I tested the back door. To my surprise, it swung open easily.

"Hello?" I called, though I knew the house was empty. "Mildred?"

My voice echoed in the silent rooms. I felt like an intruder, which, technically, I was. But concern for Mildred—and, I had to admit, curiosity about her sudden departure—overrode my usual respect for propriety.

The kitchen was just as I'd seen from the window, neat but with that one drawer open. I approached it cautiously, as if it might contain something dangerous rather than just papers.

Inside were receipts, bills, and personal correspondence—all arranged with Mildred's typical precision except for a gap where something had clearly been removed in haste. At the bottom of the drawer lay a torn envelope addressed to Mildred in elegant handwriting. The postmark was from Portland, but the return address had been torn away along with the letter it once contained. My thoughts went to Mildred's sister. Had the letter been from her? No. Judith had said the sister lived in Seattle, not Portland.

Moving to the small writing desk in the parlor, I found more evidence of hasty departure. The blotter was askew, the inkwell uncapped. Most telling of all, the drawer containing Mildred's stationery stood open, its contents disturbed as if someone had searched through them. The sheriff's deputies, most likely, but one would think they'd be less sloppy.

On the floor nearby, partially hidden under the desk, lay a crumpled piece of paper. I retrieved it, smoothing out the wrinkles to reveal part of a letter written in the same hand as the envelope.

"... cannot stress enough the importance of discretion. If anyone discovers what you've been doing, the consequences could be dire. Destroy this letter after reading and tell no one ..."

The rest was torn away, but a cold dread settled in my stomach. What had Mildred been doing? Who had written this ominous warning? And most important, had Mildred fled out of fear rather than guilt?

I folded the fragment and tucked it into my handbag. The piece was too small to be conclusive evidence of anything, but it suggested Mildred might be involved in something more complicated than a sudden family emergency.

Continuing my exploration, I made my way upstairs to Mildred's bedroom. Here, the signs of hasty packing were most evident, with a few items of clothing scattered on the bed, and a hairbrush abandoned on the vanity.

I was about to leave when something caught my eye—a small book sticking out, wedged between the mattress and headboard, as if it had slipped there accidentally during packing. I retrieved it.

It was a small leather-bound notebook, the kind Mildred used for keeping track of her piano students' progress. But when I opened it, I found something entirely different—financial records and personal notes, carefully maintained in Mildred's spidery handwriting.

At first glance, they appeared to be simple household accounts. But looking closer, there were troubling entries. Names and addresses of local families. Amounts of money beside each name, with cryptic notations like "monthly installment" and "emergency fund contribution."

There were diary entries as well. One entry caught my attention immediately:

M.A.W. says too many questions regarding payments, notably C. Butterworth musician allowances. Nobody's business.

M.A.W.—Mary Alice Wellington. And C. Butterworth was Clarence! The entry was dated just a week prior to her murder.

Another entry, more recent, read: *M.A. discussion before rehearsal. Claims she'll report concerns to Sheriff H. Tried to convince her she's misunderstanding the situation.*

My hands trembled as I turned to another page and found an entry that made my blood run cold:

Too much at stake. Meeting her tonight after practice to try one last time.

The entry ended there, dated the very day of Mary Alice's murder.

I flipped through more pages, finding detailed notes about various family situations. Information about Molly and Clarence's correspondence, about Beatrice's son Henry, about families with loved ones overseas. All of it meticulously recorded, as if Mildred had been conducting some sort of surveillance.

The implications hit me like a physical blow. What business was it of Mildred's to know people's private affairs? Was she up to something nefarious? Had Mary Alice discovered this and threatened to expose her?

A sound from downstairs—the creak of a floorboard—froze me in place. Someone had entered the house.

Clutching the notebook, I moved silently to the bedroom door, straining to hear. Soft footsteps moved through the parlor, hesitant but deliberate. Not the heavy tread of Sheriff Holcomb or his deputies. Someone trying not to be heard.

I looked frantically around the room for a hiding place or escape route. The window overlooked the front yard, too high to jump safely. The closet would be the first place anyone would check. Under the bed seemed my only option.

Crouching down, I was about to squeeze beneath the bed frame when a familiar voice called out, "Mildred? Hello? Is anyone here? It's Beatrice Fairmont."

Beatrice? What was she doing here?

Curiosity overcame caution. Tucking the notebook securely in my pocket, I straightened my skirt and cleared my throat. "Hello? Beatrice? Is that you?" I called as I descended the stairs, trying to sound surprised and innocent.

Beatrice stood in the parlor, a small basket of knitting supplies in her hands. Upon seeing me, she startled visibly, nearly dropping her basket before recovering her composure.

"Amanda! Good heavens, you gave me a fright! What are you doing here?"

"I might ask you the same thing." I choked out a light laugh. "I was just checking on Mildred's house, making sure everything was secure while she's away. Judith asked me to water her plants." The lie came distressingly easily—*Forgive me, Lord*—but it was the only excuse I could think of in the moment.

Beatrice set her basket on a side table. "How peculiar. Judith asked me to do the same thing. I suppose she asked us both to make certain someone would remember."

We regarded each other for a long moment, an awkward silence stretching between us. Beatrice was on James's list of suspects—and now here she was in another suspect's home. What did it mean, if anything?

"Well, since you're here, you can help me," I said brightly. "I can't seem to find Mildred's watering can."

"Oh, I know where they are. She keeps a couple under the kitchen sink." Beatrice moved toward the kitchen with the confidence of someone who had visited many times. "Poor Mildred, leaving in such a rush. It's not like her at all to be so disorganized."

"No, it isn't." I followed her. "Have you heard from her since she left?"

Beatrice shook her head as she knelt to open the cupboard under the sink. "Not a word." She glanced up at me.

"Her sister in Seattle must be quite ill for Mildred to leave so suddenly."

I watched her carefully. "Yes, it must be serious."

"Although . . ." Beatrice pulled out two small copper watering cans. "Between us, I think Judith misspoke. I always thought her sister lived in Portland, not Seattle. Mildred mentioned visiting her there last summer."

My pulse quickened. If Beatrice was telling the truth, then she too had noticed the discrepancy in Mildred's story. And the letter fragment I'd found could, indeed, have come from her sister. "Did she? I don't recall."

"Memory is such a tricky thing at our age." Beatrice gave a rueful smile as she filled the cans at the sink. I bristled at that remark about age—Beatrice was a good fifteen or twenty years older than I—but I let it pass. She handed me a can. "Now, you take the parlor plants, and I'll tend to the ones upstairs."

"I can help with the upstairs ones too." I was reluctant to let Beatrice out of my sight. "There are quite a few in the bedroom."

"No need to trouble yourself." Beatrice moved toward the stairs. "I've brought some of my special plant food. Mildred swears by it for her ferns."

As Beatrice disappeared upstairs, I quickly checked that Mildred's notebook was still secure in my pocket. What was Beatrice really doing here? Was she genuinely caring for a friend's plants, or searching for something as I had been?

I busied myself watering the parlor plants, straining to hear Beatrice's movements above. Floorboards creaked as she moved from room to room. Had she noticed the desk drawer I'd left open? The disturbed papers?

Eventually, Beatrice descended the stairs, the empty watering can in her hand. "All done," she announced cheerfully. "Those ferns were positively parched."

"Thank you for your help." We put the cans away, and I gathered my handbag. "I should be getting back to the shop. Molly's probably wondering where I've disappeared to."

"Such a lovely girl, your niece," Beatrice remarked as she collected her knitting basket. "My Henry always spoke highly of her."

"Yes, I remember." I'd almost forgotten that Beatrice's son had played violin in the Camp Harmony orchestra with Molly before enlisting in the military.

"Her young man is serving overseas, isn't he. Clarence, isn't it? Where is he stationed again?"

Her question took me aback. "In Europe somewhere. You know they aren't allowed to say exactly where."

"Of course. Has she heard from him lately?"

The question seemed innocent enough, but after finding Mildred's detailed notes about Clarence and Molly, I found myself on guard. "Yes, he writes regularly. Molly just received a letter last week."

"How fortunate." Beatrice sighed. "Henry's letters are so irregular. Sometimes weeks go by without a word. One can't help but worry."

"It must be difficult." A ray of genuine sympathy poked through the cloud of my suspicions. "Especially after what Mary Alice said about his service."

Beatrice's face clouded. "That was . . . unfortunate. Mary Alice didn't understand what it means to drive an ambulance under enemy fire." She shook her head. "But that's behind us now. We must focus on honoring her memory, as Eleanor Crawford suggested at rehearsal. Speaking of whom, I'm going over a bit early tonight to practice my solo with her. It's more difficult than I'd thought." Beatrice had been awarded the coveted soprano solo after Mary Alice's demise, though she had the good grace not to brag about it.

I murmured something suitably sympathetic and locked Mildred's door behind us. As we parted ways at the gate, Beatrice called after me, "Oh, Amanda? If you happen to find any of Mildred's choir music while you're checking on things, do let me know. She borrowed my copy of 'America the Beautiful' with all my markings. I'd be distressed to lose it before the concert."

"Of course," I promised. Was that what Beatrice had really been looking for upstairs? A piece of sheet music? "See you in a little while."

As I walked away, I glanced back to see her still watching me, her expression unreadable. Our encounter had done little to allay my suspicions—if anything, it had heightened them. Had she truly been there to water plants? What had she really been looking for? And had she asked those questions about Clarence out of genuine concern, or because she somehow knew about Mildred's surveillance notes?

I needed to get Mildred's notebook to James before choir practice. But as I hurried toward the sheriff's office, a new worry nagged at me. What if Beatrice told James she'd caught me snooping around Mildred's house? He'd specifically warned me not to interfere with his investigation.

The evening shadows had lengthened across Main Street by the time I reached the sheriff's office. The leather-bound notebook felt like it was burning a hole in my pocket, its damning contents weighing heavily on my mind.

Deputy Peterson was standing behind his desk when I entered, studying a map of Idaho pinned to the wall. He turned at the sound of the door.

"Miss Parrish." He placed a folder on his desk. "What can I do for you?"

"Is Sheriff Holcomb here?"

"No, he's out on a call. I wouldn't expect him back for a few hours."

I debated, then forged ahead. "I found something. Something that might be important to your investigation of the Wellington case." I avoided mentioning that it was something the deputies should have found, if they'd been thorough in their task.

He lifted an eyebrow. "That sounds ominous."

"It might be." I withdrew Mildred's notebook from my pocket and placed it on his desk. "I have reason to believe this belongs to Mildred Abernathy. The contents are . . . disturbing."

Deputy Peterson opened the notebook and scanned the first few pages, his expression growing increasingly grave. "I see what you mean. I'll see that Sheriff Holcomb gets this immediately."

I thanked the deputy and started off toward choir practice, my thoughts swirling. The notebook painted a picture of Mildred as someone who had been systematically gathering sensitive information about local families. For what purpose? Had Mary Alice discovered this scheme and paid with her life? The timing certainly suggested it was possible.

But something about it still didn't sit right with me. Mildred had always seemed so gentle, so devoted to her music and her students. True, she was something of a gossip. But could she really have been capable of both fraud and murder? And if so, where was she now? Had she fled to avoid prosecution, or was she somewhere planning her next move?

Between Mildred's apparent surveillance operation, and now Beatrice's unexpected appearance at the cottage, I felt surrounded by questions with no clear answers. The only certainty was that someone in our small community was not who they appeared to be—and that person might have blood on their hands.

Chapter Thirteen

"You're in for a treat." Eleanor guided her automobile smoothly around a curve in the road down to Coeur d'Alene. The early evening sunlight filtered through budding trees, casting dappled shadows across the countryside. "The Claybourne String Quartet is simply divine. Their interpretation of Dvořák's 'American' quartet brings tears to my eyes every time."

I adjusted my hat, still slightly self-conscious in my best blue dress. When Eleanor had appeared at my shop that morning, tickets in hand for a chamber music recital in Coeur d'Alene, I'd initially demurred.

"I couldn't possibly close the shop early," I'd protested.

"Darlin', you haven't taken a proper afternoon off since Mary Alice's funeral," Eleanor had countered, her Georgia accent thickening with persuasion. "Surely Molly can mind things for a few hours? The girl's perfectly capable."

She'd been right, of course. Molly had practically pushed me out the door, insisting she could handle any customers who might appear on a sleepy Wednesday afternoon.

"I'm embarrassed to admit I haven't attended a formal chamber music recital since my days at the conservatory," I confessed now as we drove. "I used to play the cello, until I developed a chronic wrist injury."

Eleanor's laugh was warm and free of judgment. "There's somethin' about chamber music—the intimacy of it, the conversation between instruments—that speaks to the soul in ways a full orchestra cannot."

"Like the difference between a heart-to-heart with a dear friend versus addressing a crowded room?" I suggested.

"Exactly so!" Eleanor's eyes lit up. "What a perfect analogy."

The compliment warmed me more than it should have. Since Eleanor's arrival in Timber Coulee, she'd become a bright spot in days that had grown increasingly strained following Mary Alice's murder. Her sophisticated understanding of music, her appreciation for literature, her worldly perspective—all offered welcome respite from the suffocating atmosphere of suspicion that had settled over our small town.

"Speakin' of conversations," Eleanor continued, "I've been meanin' to ask if you enjoyed *The Portrait of a Lady*? I noticed you returned it to me without comment."

"I did," I assured her. "Isabel Archer's journey was fascinating—though her choices sometimes frustrated me terribly."

"Ah! That's precisely what makes her such a compellin' character. The way she chooses the very cage she once vowed to avoid." Eleanor negotiated a sharp turn with practiced ease. "We should discuss it properly. Perhaps form a small readin' circle? I've been thinkin' Mrs. Swanson, of course. She can get us copies of the books, and she could use the distraction, her girls bein' overseas and all. And perhaps Judith Hensley? She mentioned enjoyin' Edith Wharton when we spoke at rehearsal."

"That sounds lovely." Although a small voice in my mind reminded me of the existing book club I shared with Heidi and several other local women. We'd been planning to discuss *Jane Eyre* this very evening, in fact. The realization that I'd completely forgotten our meeting sent a pang of guilt through me.

"Oh, and I almost forgot! I saw the most exquisite new milliner's shop has opened here. Perhaps we could visit it on the first Saturday in June? They're hostin' a special tea at the Desert Hotel to showcase their summer collection."

"That sounds delightful." Any opportunity to see the latest hat fashions was an immediate draw for me. Coeur d'Alene, while not a large city, offered amenities our smaller town lacked. "I could use a new summer hat."

"Splendid! It's a date, then." Eleanor guided the automobile onto Coeur d'Alene's main street, past the former Fort Sherman site. The venue for the recital—a church with elegant stained-glass windows—stood nearby, its doors already open to welcome attendees.

As Eleanor parked, several well-dressed couples made their way into the building. "I feel terribly provincial," I murmured, suddenly aware of my simple dress and last season's hat.

"Nonsense," Eleanor declared, checking her reflection in the small mirror attached to her automobile's sun visor. "You look perfectly charmin'. Besides, these small-town concerts are hardly the Metropolitan Opera. Half the audience will be loggers who've put on their Sunday best."

She wasn't entirely correct—the attendees appeared to be primarily from Coeur d'Alene's upper echelon—but her reassurance buoyed my confidence as we entered the church. The interior had been transformed into an intimate concert hall, with rows of chairs arranged in a semicircle around a small stage where four chairs and music stands awaited the performers.

Eleanor guided me to seats near the front, nodding graciously to several acquaintances along the way. I followed, wondering how she'd managed to forge connections in Coeur d'Alene when she'd been in the area for such a short time.

"Do you know many people here?" I whispered as we settled into our seats.

"Just a few," she replied. "When one travels as much as I have, one learns to make acquaintances quickly." She leaned closer as if telling a secret. "Though between us, I find the society here refreshingly unpretentious compared to places like Atlanta or Charleston."

The lights dimmed before I could respond, and the quartet entered to polite applause. They took their places—two violinists, a violist, and a cellist—and began with a Mozart piece that filled the space with bright, precise harmonies.

The music transported me, much as Eleanor had promised. The interplay between instruments created a tapestry of sound more intricate and personal than anything I'd experienced before. When they began the Dvořák piece Eleanor had mentioned, I understood why she'd been so enthusiastic. The music captured something quintessentially American while remaining firmly rooted in European traditions—a melding of worlds that created something entirely new.

During intermission, Eleanor introduced me to several people, including the director of the Coeur d'Alene Musical Society, who expressed interest in having Mountain Melodies supply sheet music for their educational programs.

"You see?" Eleanor murmured as we returned to our seats for the second half. "Connections are bein' forged. Business opportunities present themselves in the most unexpected places."

The remainder of the concert passed in a blur of beautiful sound and emotional resonance. As we drove back to Timber Coulee under a canopy of stars, I felt nourished in a way that went beyond the physical—as if my soul had been fed after a long period of hunger.

"Thank you," I said. "You were right. I needed this."

"We all need beauty, especially in difficult times." Eleanor's gentle voice filled the darkness of the automobile. "Art and music aren't luxuries—they're essential nourishment."

"Like literature," I agreed, thinking of our earlier conversation. "I shall look forward to the reading circle."

"Then it's settled." Eleanor slowed as we approached the outskirts of Timber Coulee. "I'll speak with Judith and Mrs. Swanson tomorrow. Perhaps we could meet on Monday at the Hummingbird Tearoom? Say, noon?"

"That sounds perfect." A pleasant anticipation buoyed me at the prospect.

As Eleanor pulled up in front of my cottage, I felt a curious reluctance to end our outing. The evening had offered such a welcome respite from the tensions and worries of recent weeks.

"Would you like to come in for tea?" I offered on impulse. "Molly's likely still awake."

"That's very sweet of you, sugar, but I should be gettin' back to the hotel. I have an article deadline loomin'." Eleanor leaned over to give my hand a warm squeeze. "But I'll see you at choir practice tomorrow."

As her automobile disappeared down Main Street, I was struck by how quickly Eleanor Crawford had become a fixture in my life. In the short weeks since her arrival, she'd brought music, literature, and a renewed sense of purpose to my days. Only her apparent interest in James Holcomb left me feeling a bit unsettled. But that might have simply been her naturally flirtatious manner.

It wasn't until I was preparing for bed that I remembered, with a sudden stab of guilt, the book club meeting I'd missed. Heidi would be disappointed, particularly since I'd been the one to suggest reading *Jane Eyre*. I made a mental note to stop by her shop tomorrow with an apology and explanation.

Though, I reflected as I extinguished my bedside lamp, how could I explain the sense of intellectual awakening Eleanor's friendship had sparked? Heidi was a dear friend, of course, but our connection had always been more practical than philosophical.

Perhaps I could find a way to include her in some of these new activities. Yes, I decided as sleep began to claim me, I would invite Heidi to the new literary circle. And perhaps to the milliner's shop in Coeur d'Alene in June as well. After all, friendships shouldn't be exclusive affairs.

With that comforting resolution, I drifted off to sleep, the echoes of Dvořák's quartet still playing softly in my mind.

Chapter Fourteen

T he following Monday, I'd just returned from a lively book discussion with Eleanor, Judith, and Ruth Swanson at the Hummingbird Tearoom and was checking my inventory of violin strings when Heidi dropped in, carrying a guitar.

"Somebody donated this old thing to Elite Repeat." She referred to her secondhand shop. "You have better results selling used musical instruments than I do. Do you want it?"

"Thanks. I'll take a look at it. If I can't use it, maybe Camp Harmony can give it a good home." I took the guitar from her and gave it an experimental strum. Not too bad. The tone had a pleasant mellowness that suggested quality underneath its worn appearance.

She lingered after I'd set the guitar aside, wandering around the shop and adjusting displays that didn't need adjusting. "So, Judith tells me Eleanor's organizing a new literary society."

"She has, at least for as long as she's here in town. We met for the first time today, in fact." A sudden sense of regret washed over me. "I'm sorry. I meant to invite you and forgot all about it. Next time, for sure." I returned to my inventory list.

"How thoughtful of her to include you." Heidi's voice held an edge I couldn't quite identify. "Though I suppose it makes sense, given your friendship."

I looked up, catching something in her tone.

"And she couldn't have found a better reading companion." Heidi picked up a harmonica, examined it, and put it back. "You two have become quite inseparable these days."

The shop had been unusually busy since reopening after Mary Alice's murder. Morbid curiosity, I supposed. People wanting to see where it happened, perhaps hoping to glimpse some evidence that might confirm their own theories. Heidi, however, seemed to be here for a different reason entirely.

"Eleanor's been a comfort during a difficult time." I chose my words with care, not sure what she was insinuating.

"Mmm," Heidi hummed noncommittally. "Like spending over an hour at the tearoom today debating the merits of Henry James."

I stiffened. "News travels fast."

"I was there," she said, "sitting at a table behind you. Not that any of you noticed."

"You were there? You should have joined us."

"Wouldn't want to intrude." Was that it? Was Heidi miffed she hadn't been invited to join the group? She examined a bow as if checking for flaws. "But people notice, you know, when the music shop closes for an extended break in the middle of the day."

"I left a note on the door." My defensive spirit rose. "And Molly was here all morning."

"I'm not criticizing your business practices, Amanda." Heidi set the bow down with deliberate care. "I just find it curious how quickly Eleanor has become your literary confidante. I didn't realize you were so passionate about Henry James."

"We'd all read *The Portrait of a Lady*." Why was I feeling so defensive? "We were discussing the protagonist's choices."

"How fascinating." Heidi's voice was strained despite her smile. "And what about our book club meeting you missed last week? We were discussing *Jane Eyre*—a novel you specifically requested."

I winced, genuinely remorseful. "I'm sorry about that. Eleanor had tickets to a chamber music recital in Coeur d'Alene, and it completely slipped my mind."

"A chamber music recital," Heidi repeated flatly. "Well, I can't say I would have enjoyed sitting through hours of highbrow music. Sounds dull."

Not that I'd asked for her opinion. "It wasn't like that at all. The music was emotional, powerful—it spoke directly to the heart."

"And I suppose Eleanor was the perfect companion for such an enlightening event."

"She was," I confirmed, ignoring the sharpness in Heidi's tone. "She knows so much about classical compositions. It helped me appreciate nuances I might have missed otherwise."

"How fortunate for you to have found someone so . . . educational." Heidi examined her fingernail. "Speaking of Coeur d'Alene, there's a big estate sale down there on the first Saturday in June. I thought we might go together, like we used to. Quite the collection of vintage instruments, from what I hear. Might be some good finds for both our shops."

The invitation caught me at a disadvantage. Heidi and I had indeed made a tradition of attending local estate sales together, often making a day of it with luncheon at whatever small café we could find. In the past, I'd always looked forward to these outings.

"Oh, I'm not sure I can." A sudden awkwardness settled over me. "Eleanor mentioned possibly visiting a new milliner's shop that day."

Hurt, quickly masked by indifference, flickered across Heidi's face. "More educational experiences, I'm sure. Well, it was just a thought."

"Come with us," I urged. "It'll be fun, the three of us."

"I think not."

"We'll watch for another estate sale, then?" The offer sounded hollow even to my own ears.

"Of course." Heidi moved to another display, her back to me. "Whenever you're not busy with Eleanor."

The emphasis she placed on Eleanor's name carried an unmistakable note of resentment. I set down my pencil, my defensiveness surging. "Is there something you want to say, Heidi?"

She ignored my question. "Oh, she's charming, of course, but don't you find it odd how she appeared out of nowhere at exactly the right moment? Almost as if she were waiting in the wings."

I stared at her. "What are you suggesting?"

Heidi lowered her voice. "I'm not suggesting anything, exactly. But the timing is peculiar, isn't it? Mary Alice is murdered, Mildred vanishes, and suddenly this Southern journalist who happens to play piano is available to step in."

"Eleanor has nothing to do with any of this," I said sharply. "She's been a godsend for the choir and for this town."

Heidi blinked. "Well, you don't have to get all defensive about it. I wasn't accusing her of anything."

"Weren't you? Mentioning her in the same breath as Mary Alice's murder sounds like an accusation to me."

"I didn't say that," Heidi protested, though her expression suggested otherwise. "I'm just pointing out that we know almost nothing about her. She sweeps into town with her honeyed accent and musical talents, and suddenly everyone's falling all over themselves to welcome her."

"Perhaps because she's genuinely warm and talented," I retorted. "Not everyone needs to live in a place for thirty years to be accepted."

Heidi's cheeks flushed. "That's not fair, Amanda. I'm just being cautious. After what happened to Mary Alice—"

"What happened to Mary Alice has nothing to do with Eleanor. She didn't even know Mary Alice!"

"So she claims," Heidi muttered.

I slapped my ledger book closed. "I won't listen to this, Heidi. Eleanor has been nothing but kind and supportive during this terrible time. Ad unlike some people, she doesn't spend her time spreading unfounded suspicions about newcomers."

"Unlike some people?" Heidi's eyes narrowed. "Is that what you think I'm doing? Being a gossip?"

"If the shoe fits."

"Well!" Heidi drew herself up indignantly. "I'm sorry my decade of friendship doesn't measure up to your new best friend from Georgia. I suppose Eleanor's fancy book discussions are more stimulating than my little secondhand shop stories."

So that was it. "This isn't about Eleanor at all, is it? You're jealous."

"Jealous?" Heidi sputtered. "That's ridiculous! Why would I be jealous of someone I barely know?"

"Because I've spent time with her. Because we have things in common."

"Oh yes, your shared love of music and literature," Heidi said with uncharacteristic bitterness. "I've only heard about it a dozen times. 'Eleanor recommended the most fascinating book.' 'Eleanor plays Chopin like an angel.' I'm surprised you have time for your old friends with your packed social calendar."

I was taken aback by her vehemence. "That's not fair, Heidi. I've hardly seen you these past weeks except at choir."

"I stopped by three times! You were either closed or rushing off to meet Eleanor."

Had I really been neglecting my old friend that much? A sharp pang of guilt was quickly overwhelmed by indignation at her unfair suspicions of Eleanor.

"I'm sorry if you feel neglected, but that doesn't give you the right to cast aspersions on Eleanor. She's been through enough, losing her husband in the war."

"If he even existed," Heidi muttered.

"What did you say?" I demanded, shocked by her insinuation.

"Nothing." Heidi picked up her handbag. "I can see you're determined to believe the best of your new friend, regardless of the circumstances. Just don't come crying to me when she disappoints you."

"Eleanor is genuine, kind, and talented. I won't hear another word against her."

"Fine." Heidi moved toward the door. "I hope for your sake you're right. But ask yourself this—have you actually verified anything she's told you? About her husband? Her journalism career? Anything at all?"

"I don't need to verify what a friend tells me," I replied coldly. "That's what friendship means—trust."

"Trust has to be earned, Amanda." Heidi paused at the door. "Eleanor may be a wonderful pianist and the most charming woman in Georgia, but that doesn't mean she is who she claims to be. Even Sarah would have asked questions."

The mention of Sarah stung like a slap. "Don't you dare bring Sarah into this."

"Someone needs to," Heidi retorted. "She wouldn't have let a pretty accent blind her to common sense."

"Get out." My voice shook with anger. "Get out of my shop."

Heidi's face fell, as if she realized she'd gone too far. "Amanda, I—"

"Now, please."

"But it's Monday. There's a rehearsal tonight—"

"Heidi, please. I can't keep talking to you right now. I need to think. To cool down."

Without another word, Heidi slipped out the door, leaving me trembling with fury. How dare she imply that Eleanor was somehow involved in Mary Alice's murder? How dare she question the existence of Eleanor's dead husband? And to bring Sarah into it—that was beyond the pale.

Eleanor had been nothing but kindness personified since arriving in Timber Coulee. If Heidi couldn't see that, if she was so blinded by petty jealousy that she needed to invent sinister motives for Eleanor's presence in town, then perhaps our friendship wasn't as strong as I'd believed.

The shop door swung open as another customer entered, forcing me to compose myself and paste on a professional smile. But inside, I was seething.

And as for Heidi's parting shot about "verifying" Eleanor's stories—what nonsense. Eleanor Crawford was exactly who she appeared to be—a talented, educated Southern lady who had suffered her own war losses and now sought to bring comfort through her music and writing.

Anyone who couldn't see that was simply not looking hard enough.

Chapter Fifteen

The next day, I felt terrible about my argument with Heidi. She was my good friend, after all, and had been a part of my Timber Coulee story practically from the beginning. Maybe we didn't spend a lot of time together, and maybe we didn't have as many interests in common as Sarah and I had years ago, or as Eleanor and I did now, but even so, I hadn't meant to neglect her or make her feel left out. At the very least, as fellow Main Street business owners and members of the Chamber of Commerce, our paths would continue to cross at regular intervals. We needed to clear the air.

I'd planned to speak to her at the previous night's choir rehearsal, but she hadn't shown up. I had, however, gotten some answers concerning Beatrice Fairmont. For one, Judith confirmed she had, indeed, asked Beatrice to water Mildred's plants, so her presence in the cottage—unlike mine—was legitimate. For another, Beatrice located her missing copy of 'America the Beautiful' lying loose amid the stack of music folders, where it had apparently slipped out of her own, so Mildred hadn't taken it, after all. I made a mental note to share these details with James at the earliest opportunity.

That opportunity came sooner than expected. I was just about to pick up the telephone to call Heidi when it jangled. I reached for it, hoping it was Heidi calling, a heartfelt apology forming on my tongue.

"Sheriff Holcomb on the line," the operator rasped.

"Amanda? It's James. I'd like to talk to you about this notebook you dropped off."

His cool, even tone gave me no hint as to whether or not he was annoyed with me.

"Certainly. Would you mind coming here? Or better yet, come by for supper after work. Molly's been practicing a mushroom stroganoff recipe from the Food Administration's *Victory Cookbook.*"

"I'm looking forward to it."

I bet he was. But whether he looked forward to enjoying Molly's beefless stroganoff, or to quizzing me about Mildred's notebook, I hadn't the faintest idea.

After concluding the call, I asked the operator to connect me with Heidi's number. I let the number ring and ring until the operator was forced to state the obvious. "There's no answer."

After closing the shop, I hurried home. Molly had been hard at work in the kitchen, and the place already smelled savory and tantalizing.

I took some time to fix my hair and change clothes, choosing a white cotton dress embroidered with yellow daisies that I happened to know James liked. When he arrived, I motioned to the armchair while I took the sofa. He sat upright, every inch the professional lawman. He opened his briefcase, pulled out Mildred's notebook, and laid it on the table between us. I pointed to it.

"Have you had time to read it?"

"I have." He made no move to touch the notebook. "And how, exactly, did it come into your possession?" His voice held that careful neutrality I'd come to recognize as his "sheriff tone"—the one that warned me I might be stepping over a line.

I hesitated, then decided honesty was the only path forward. "I went to Mildred's cottage." Then honesty took a detour out the window. "To water her plants."

"At whose request?"

"No one's," I admitted. "I was concerned about her sudden departure. It seemed . . . out of character."

James sighed, the sound weary but not entirely surprised. "Amanda, we've discussed this. You can't just—"

"The back door was unlocked," I continued quickly before he could build up steam. "The house showed signs of someone leaving in a hurry. And I found that notebook wedged between the mattress and headboard. As your deputies should have." I slid him a glance, gauging his reaction to this slur on his investigation, but his face remained impassive. "It sounds like Mildred was helping Mary Alice in some way. There are entries about Mary Alice, about her suspicion of fraud in the Ladies' Aid Society accounts."

"And did you find it before or after Beatrice Fairmont arrived?" he asked in a dry tone.

I blinked in surprise. "How did you—"

"Mrs. Fairmont reported it herself," he said. "She mentioned running into you while supposedly watering plants, though she didn't mention breaking and entering. Just how thirsty were these plants, anyway?"

My cheeks warmed. "I didn't break anything. The door was unlocked."

"Still entering without permission."

"I didn't think Beatrice had permission either," I pointed out. "She claimed Judith Hensley asked her to water the plants, but something about her story didn't ring true. But later, Judith confirmed it, so she was telling the truth. But about Mildred's observations—"

He picked up the notebook and flipped it open. "Go on."

"You've seen the private financial details. Suspicious, right?" When he didn't respond, I moved closer, pointing to the relevant entry while being careful not to crowd him. "And look at this entry from the day after Mary Alice's murder."

James read it aloud. "'She knows I've seen the books. Not safe here anymore. P. says come immediately.'" He looked up at me. "We don't know who 'she' is. And who's this 'P'?"

"Possibly her sister. And there's more." I described finding the torn letter fragment and detailed Beatrice's unexpected appearance at the cottage—her strange questions about Clarence and her particular interest in going upstairs alone.

"Did you notice anything unusual about her behavior?" James asked.

"I don't know. She seemed too interested in Mildred's bedroom. And when she asked about Clarence's letters, there was something in her tone I didn't like." I frowned. "You don't think Beatrice could be involved in this, do you?"

James shook his head. "I've already cleared Mrs. Fairmont as a suspect in Mary Alice's murder. She was at the hospital with her aunt when the murder occurred—three witnesses have confirmed it. What we're looking for now is any possible information she might have about Mildred Abernathy's whereabouts, the financial details, or anything else connected to this case. What else can you tell me about your encounter?"

"She said she was hoping to find a missing music score that Mildred might have borrowed, which is plausible. She did misplace it, and later it turned up in the rehearsal room. But again, I don't know if that's the sole reason for her interest in poking around Mildred's house."

"That," James said, "is what I intend to find out."

"I found something else." I retrieved the letter fragment from my handbag. "It's not much, but it seems to corroborate what's in the notebook."

He examined the paper scrap. "'If anyone discovers what you've been doing, the consequences could be dire,'" he read aloud. "No signature."

"The rest was torn away. Beatrice mentioned thinking Mildred's sister lived in Portland, not Seattle. And I did find a matching envelope with a Portland postmark, but no return address."

James looked thoughtful. "Let's see. Sterling City," he murmured. "Millbrook. Portland." He ticked off each town on his fingers. "Each town has had a murder or violent crime in the past six months. Each victim was connected to the war effort, particularly to financial support for soldiers or their families."

Dread coiled in my belly. "You think there's some connection?"

"I think it's a possibility we can't ignore."

We sat in silence for a moment, the implications settling between us like a physical weight. Outside, lamplight illuminated the empty street. In the distance, a piano played—someone practicing for the upcoming patriotic concert, perhaps.

An unwelcome suspicion took shape in my mind, hazy at first, then clearer, like a camera lens coming into focus . "Eleanor was asking questions about families, too," I blurted. "She seemed particularly interested in how families receive military allotments."

James scowled. "When did this happen"

I recounted our conversation at the Hummingbird Tearoom—Eleanor's questions about support groups for military families, her interest in financial arrangements.

"She also made comments specifically about Viola's brother." The memory returned with new significance. All the while, the creeping notion that perhaps she was connected to the crime somehow—that Heidi had been right—formed a rock in the pit of my stomach.

"Interesting timing." James made another note.

"She mentioned being an Army wife. Said her husband died in France last year. Walter Crawford, an engineer."

James wrote that down, too. "I'll have Deputy Peterson wire the War Department to verify that."

"You don't think she's who she claims to be?" Even as I asked, the tiniest tentacles of suspicion crept into my mind. Eleanor's smooth insertion into our community through the choir. Her detailed questions about military families.

But she was my friend.

"I don't know," James admitted. "But her credentials are vague at best."

I felt a flicker of defensiveness on Eleanor's behalf. "She's been nothing but kind and supportive since I met her. She's helped the choir heal after Mary Alice's death." I couldn't bring myself to mention how she helped me heal, too. The creeping suspicion that she might not be who I thought she was filled me with despair.

"Kindness can be a very effective cover, Amanda." James voice was gentle. "I'm not accusing her of anything. But the timing of her arrival, combined with her interest in military families and her connection to the choir—the very group Mary Alice was part of when she was killed—raises questions we need to consider."

My stomach knotted as I remembered how easily I'd welcomed Eleanor, how quickly I'd shared information about Molly's beau and other soldiers' families. "If she is involved in this fraud scheme . . ."

"Then we need to be very careful," James finished. "Especially now that we have this." He tapped Mildred's notebook. "This is evidence that could prove damaging to whoever is behind this scheme."

The ordinary brown book took on new significance. "What should we do?"

"I'll communicate with the sheriffs in Sterling City and those other jurisdictions. Compare notes on their cases. And I'll need to speak with Pearl Pritchard about those financial discrepancies." He rubbed his temples, a gesture I recognized from our years of friendship. It meant he was overtaxed, possibly overlooking something.

"I should also follow up again with Beatrice Fairmont," he added. "While she's been cleared of Mary Alice's murder, her presence at Mildred's cottage raises new questions. She might have information that could help us locate Mildred."

Before I could think better of it, I touched his arm. "James, you can't do this alone. Let me help. The choir trusts me, and Eleanor does too—at least for now."

He stiffened slightly at my touch, then relaxed. "It's too dangerous, Amanda. If Eleanor is involved, and if she realizes you suspect her . . ."

"I'll be careful," I promised. "Besides, I'm in a position to notice things you might not. I'll start by finding out what I can about the magazine she works for and make sure she's a legitimate journalist. I'm sure she is, but it will be good to know for certain."

James looked down at my hand still resting on his arm. For a moment, I thought he might cover it with his own. Instead, he stood and resumed his professional demeanor, though his eyes remained troubled.

"Very well. But you'll report anything unusual to me immediately. No investigating on your own." His voice softened. "I couldn't bear it if anything happened to you, Amanda."

The words hung between us, weighted with unspoken grief and possibilities neither of us had been brave enough to acknowledge. Sarah's spirit seemed to stand with us in that moment—not as a barrier, but as a witness to how life continues even after profound loss.

"I'll be careful." My voice came out barely above a whisper.

"See that you are." He cleared his throat.

"Supper's ready," Molly called from the kitchen, breaking the awkward moment. We settled around the table, the silence punctuated only by the clinking of silverware against plates. James complimented Molly's stroganoff, which normally would have brightened her countenance. Tonight, however, she merely nodded, her gaze fixed on her plate.

Whatever was the matter with my niece? From the slight tremor in her hands as she reached for her water glass, something weighed on her, something beyond the obvious stress of being a murder suspect.

"Molly," James said calmly, setting down his fork, "I'm sorry. I need to ask you again. Where were you after you left Viola's house that night?"

Molly's shoulders stiffened. She glanced at me, then back at James, her expression conflicted. Then her shoulders dropped into a slump. "I wasn't just walking home," she whispered. Finally, she seemed ready to tell the truth! I braced myself for what she might say next. "I went to the Timber Coulee Hotel."

James raised an eyebrow but said nothing, giving her space to continue.

"When I was walking Viola home, she was so distressed about Edward. She kept saying the letter about his gambling debts couldn't be true." Molly took a shaky breath.

"She mentioned that Edward's friend Tommy Morrison was back in town, working as a night bellhop at the hotel. Edward had told her if anything ever seemed wrong, to talk to Tommy."

"And you went to find him?" I asked gently.

She nodded. "Viola was too distraught to go herself, and I thought . . . I thought if I could just talk to Tommy, maybe he'd know something that could help the Thorntons. I found him at the service entrance—he was just getting off his shift."

James leaned forward slightly. "What did Tommy Morrison tell you?"

"He was nervous." Molly toyed with the stem of her water goblet. "He made me promise not to tell anyone we'd spoken." She slid a glance to the sheriff. "Tommy and Edward and some of the other boys like to gamble and play cards. It's supposed to be a secret—you know, like a secret club."

"Don't worry," James assured her. "The sheriff's office is aware this goes on, and we've been monitoring the situation. So far it seems like harmless fun."

"Well, not so harmless for Edward," Molly continued. "It seems he wanted to play for bigger and bigger stakes—even went to Spokane to try his luck there. Tommy confirmed that Edward did have gambling problems before enlisting—that's why his parents were so quick to believe the letter."

"But he doesn't anymore?" I prompted.

"No. According to Tommy, Edward swore off gambling completely after almost losing the family's wagon team in a card game last year. He did owe a debt—a big one—to some tough guy over in Spokane, but that situation brought him to his senses." Molly's words came faster now. "Tommy said Edward has been completely clean since joining up—he even refuses friendly card games with no stakes involved."

James and I exchanged glances. "Then the letter must be fraudulent," I said.

"Tommy thinks someone in town must be using Edward's past to target his family," Molly continued. "Someone who knows about his history and has access to military letterhead. It's not exactly a secret. He said Mrs. Crawford has seemed kind of nosy, too, asking him questions about which local boys had 'problems' before enlisting. He likes talking to her because she tips him handsomely, but he doesn't like all her questions."

James's demeanor sharpened. "Mrs. Crawford specifically asked about soldiers with troubled pasts?"

Molly nodded. "Tommy said she was especially interested in boys with gambling debts or other financial troubles.

Anyway, he's afraid that soon the whole town will know about the gambling club and he'll lose his job, and the other boys will accuse him of squealing, and maybe even that gangster fellow in Spokane will hear about it, which could spell real trouble for Tommy." Molly paused to take a sip of water.

"Go on," James encouraged, his supper now apparently forgotten. "Tell me more about this fellow in Spokane."

"Well, before Edward went overseas, he told Tommy he paid back every cent he owed this man." Molly's voice dropped low. "But then that threatening letter came."

"So that's why you took so long that night?" I asked. "You were talking to Tommy?"

Her face reddened. "Yes, but there's something else. After I finished talking to Tommy, I was heading through the lobby to leave when I saw . . . someone. A well-dressed man at the front desk, asking for Eleanor Crawford. It was very late at night."

James stopped his hand mid-reach for his water glass. "Did you hear a name?"

"No. The desk clerk said Mrs. Crawford had been out all evening and hadn't returned, but the man kept insisting. I couldn't make out his words, but they must have been persuasive, because the next thing I knew, he was headed for the elevator, I assume going up to Mrs. Crawford's room."

Molly's eyes focused on some distant point. "He passed right by me and pulled out a cigarette case, and when he lit his cigarette, there was this peculiar, spicy smell. Like incense, almost. I don't know why, but something about him made me uneasy. Maybe because he was arguing with the clerk, or the way he kept looking around the lobby like he expected to be followed. I decided to wait and see if he'd come back down."

"Did he?" James's tone was now fully professional.

"Yes. He was carrying a leather portfolio that he didn't have before." Molly bit her lip. "And he looked . . . satisfied. Like he'd concluded successful business."

"Why didn't you tell me this before, Miss Mulroney?" James's tone held concern rather than accusation.

Tears welled in Molly's eyes. "Because the next morning, Mary Alice was dead. And when you started asking about my whereabouts, I panicked. How could I explain that I'd been sneaking around alleys, spying on hotel guests? And if I mentioned Tommy, he could lose his job—or worse. He made me promise. He said these people were dangerous."

I reached across the table to squeeze her hand. "It's all right." But was is? My pulse quickened. Molly had witnessed someone exchanging what might have been private information—or who knows what else—on the very night Mary Alice was murdered.

James pushed back from the table, his expression grave but thoughtful. "Miss Mulroney, this information could be vital to our investigation. Tommy Morrison's testimony about Edward Thornton's past gambling problems provides context for why the Thorntons were targeted. And your description of the man visiting Mrs. Crawford matches other reports we've received."

"You won't tell anyone about Tommy, will you?" Molly asked anxiously. "He's terrified of losing his position—his mother depends on his income—and also he's afraid of that gangster in Spokane."

"I'll be discreet," James promised. "But I will need to speak with him."

Molly nodded, relief evident in her posture. The remainder of our meal passed in thoughtful silence.

When we'd finished dessert and James got up to leave, I walked him to the door, suddenly aware of how the evening's revelations had changed everything.

"What about the notebook?" I asked quietly.

"I'll keep it secure." He scooped it up from the table and tucking it in his briefcase. "Molly's account adds another crucial piece to this puzzle. The timing of that man's visit to Eleanor Crawford, combined with what we know about the fraudulent letter to the Thorntons—"

"Do you think," I interrupted him, "that Mary Alice discovered their connection? That Eleanor might have been gathering information about vulnerable families?"

"It's possible." James's mouth pulled down into a grim line. "And if she confronted her about it . . ." He didn't need to finish the thought.

"And Beatrice?"

"I suspect there's no malice in Mrs. Fairmont's intentions—just a mother desperate for information about her son."

The way Beatrice had bristled when Mary Alice belittled Henry's service . . . perhaps her actions, however questionable, came from a place I could understand all too well—the need to protect someone she loved.

James patted the notebook. "Thank you for bringing this to me." A smile tugged at one corner of his mouth. "Even if your methods were somewhat . . . unorthodox."

"Nothing about this case has been orthodox." I returned his almost-smile with one of my own.

As he turned to leave, he called back to me. "Amanda? Lock your doors tonight—every night. And keep Molly close." The gravity in his voice sent a fresh wave of dread through me. Unable to find words that wouldn't betray my growing fear, I settled for a nod.

Outside, the evening had deepened into true night. The street lamps cast pools of light that seemed more like islands in a dangerous sea than beacons of safety. And for the first time since Mary Alice's murder, I truly understood why Mildred had fled in the night, leaving everything behind.

As I closed and locked the door, I was torn between loyalty to my new friend and the disturbing implications of James's suspicions. Eleanor had been a bright spot in these dark days—supportive, understanding, and seemingly genuine in her concern. Could she really be involved in something so sinister? I didn't want to believe it. But her convenient arrival, her immediate interest in our military families, her vague credentials, and now this mysterious nighttime visitor . . . doubts crept in like a cold draft under a door. As I returned to the kitchen where Molly was washing dishes, I paused with one hand steadying myself in the doorway.

Had Mary Alice discovered the same connection that night? Had she pieced together that Eleanor might be somehow involved in an endeavor not entirely above-board? And most chillingly—had she confronted her about it, sealing her own fate?

After all, according to what Molly overheard the desk clerk say, it did not appear Eleanor was in the hotel at the time Mary Alice was killed.

Chapter Sixteen

The skies over Timber Coulee had finally cleared after three days of gloomy spring rain. Golden morning light spilled through the high windows of Swanson's Bookstore as I pushed open the door. The shop was pleasantly quiet, with just the gentle rustle of pages being turned and the occasional murmur of conversation.

Ruth Swanson and her assistant were restocking a display of the latest Zane Grey novel. She looked up and smiled when she saw me.

"Amanda! What a pleasant surprise. I don't often see you in here on a Saturday morning."

"Good morning, Ruth." I weaved my way through the stacks toward her. "The shop isn't busy, so I left Molly in charge for an hour. I wanted to check if that new women's magazine has come in yet. Molly said she talked to you about ordering it."

Ruth's smile faded slightly. "Oh dear. I was going to telephone you about that today." She straightened up from her crouched position, setting down the books she had been arranging. "Why don't you come into the back room? I've just made a pot of tea. Glenda, will you take over for a few minutes?"

The assistant nodded. A small flutter of unease stirred in my chest as I followed Ruth through the curtained doorway that separated the shop floor from her small office. Something in her tone suggested this wasn't going to be a simple "it hasn't arrived yet" conversation.

The back room was cozy and cluttered in the best possible way—stacks of catalogs and publishers' notices covered every surface, and the walls were lined with shelves containing books that hadn't yet made it to the shop floor. It took every ounce of my self-discipline not to scan the titles and start leafing through them. Ruth gestured for me to take a seat in a worn leather armchair while she poured two cups of tea.

"I feel terrible." She handed me a steaming cup. "I've spent the past two weeks trying to track down copies of *Angel of the Hearth* for you and Molly, but I've hit something of a wall."

"It hasn't come in with your regular shipment?" I already suspected the answer would be more complicated than that.

"Amanda." Ruth settled into her own chair with a sigh, "I can't find any evidence that the magazine exists at all."

Though James's questions had already planted seeds of doubt, hearing it confirmed sent a chill through me that had nothing to do with the spring morning.

"What do you mean?" I braced myself for an answer I didn't really want to hear.

"At first, I thought perhaps it was just a small publication, or a regional one I hadn't encountered before." Ruth took a sip of her tea. "That happens sometimes—literary journals from universities, or specialty magazines with limited circulation. But I've been a bookseller for thirty years, and I pride myself on being able to find just about anything in print."

She reached for a folder on her desk and opened it, revealing a stack of correspondence. "I asked every distributor in my network. I telephoned Johnson & Sons in Chicago, Caldwell's in Denver, even Riverdale Press in New Orleans, thinking perhaps it was a Southern publication." She spread the letters on the small table between us. "Every single one came back with the same answer—they've never heard of it."

I picked up one of the replies, scanning the typewritten text. "We regret to inform you that we have no record of any publication titled *Angel of the Hearth* in our current or back catalogs . . ."

"I even telegraphed my cousin Margaret in Atlanta," Ruth continued, "since your friend Mrs. Crawford mentioned growing up in Georgia. Margaret belongs to three different women's literary societies. She's never heard of it either."

"Could it be very new?" I suggested, grasping at straws. "Perhaps it hasn't been widely distributed yet."

"I thought of that," Ruth nodded. "So I rang up *Publishers Weekly* for their listing of new periodicals. Nothing." She hesitated, looking genuinely regretful. "I'm afraid, my dear, that either this magazine exists under another name that your friend has confused, or—"

"Or it doesn't exist at all." I finished her thought.

She didn't respond, but her expression was full of sympathy. We both knew what this might mean.

I stared into my teacup, watching the amber liquid swirl as my mind raced through implications. If Eleanor had lied about writing for this magazine, what else had she lied about? Her supposed journalism career was the foundation of her presence in Timber Coulee—her entire reason for being here.

"Did she show you any of her articles?" Ruth asked gently.

I shook my head. "She promised to send copies to Judith Hensley for the article about women's fashion during wartime. But I've never actually seen one myself." Another thought struck me. "In fact, I realized I've never seen her writing anything at all. No notes, no drafts . . ." I set down my teacup with slightly too much force, causing a small splash. "What kind of journalist doesn't write?"

Ruth reached out and patted my hand. "I'm sorry, Amanda. I know you've become friends with Mrs. Crawford. And I did enjoy our book discussion the other day. I can see why you like her."

"Yes," I affirmed, though the word felt hollow now. *Friend*. I'd opened my heart to Eleanor, shared confidences, even defended her against Heidi's suspicions. And all the while, she'd been . . . what? Lying? Pretending?

But why? What possible reason could a woman have for fabricating an entire career, an entire publication?

Unless . . .

Mary Alice's murder. The missing war relief funds. The odd questions about military families. Mildred's sudden departure. And what James had said about a certain crime in Sterling City , , ,

Pieces were clicking into place like a kaleidoscope, forming a picture I didn't want to see.

"Amanda?" Ruth was watching me with concern. "Are you all right? You've gone quite pale."

I arranged my features into a smile. "I'm fine. Just . . . surprised. And wondering why someone would claim to write for a magazine that doesn't exist."

"Perhaps it's an innocent misunderstanding," Ruth suggested, though her tone suggested she didn't believe it any more than I did.

"Perhaps." I stood. "Thank you for going to so much trouble, Ruth. I appreciate your thoroughness."

"Of course, dear. Would you like me to keep trying? There are a few more avenues I could explore."

"No." My response shot out a little too quickly. "No, you've done more than enough. I'll simply ask Eleanor about it directly."

Though I had no intention of doing any such thing. If Eleanor Crawford—if that was even her real name—was hiding something, the last thing I wanted was to alert her that I was growing suspicious.

As I stepped back onto Main Street, the cheerful spring morning seemed at odds with the dark thoughts churning in my mind. I'd been so eager for friendship, so desperate for a connection to fill the void left by Sarah's death, that I'd overlooked what should have been obvious warning signs.

The elegant clothes that seemed beyond a journalist's salary. The vague references to her past. The probing questions about military families.

I needed to tell James about this new discovery. But first, I had to make things right with someone who had tried to warn me all along.

Chapter Seventeen

The Hummingbird Cafe bustled with a Saturday crowd—weary shoppers taking a rest, ladies from the church auxiliary planning their next bake sale, and Charlie Talbott behind the counter, somehow managing to keep everyone's orders straight without writing anything down.

I spotted Heidi at a corner table by the window, her honey-blonde hair catching the sunlight. She looked up as I approached, her expression polite but guarded.

My stomach twisted with guilt.

"I ordered you a blackberry scone," she said as I slid into the chair across from her. "And tea with honey, the way you like it."

"Thank you." I removed my gloves. "That's very thoughtful."

An awkward silence settled between us. Earlier that week, we'd had our first real argument in over a decade of friendship. The memory of her hurt expression as she'd stormed out of Mountain Melodies still made me wince. It had been the right thing to do to telephone her and invite her for tea, and a relief when she accepted.

"Heidi, I—" "Amanda, I want to—"

We both spoke at once, then stopped, exchanging small smiles that eased some of the tension.

"Please." I gestured for her to continue.

She twisted her napkin between her fingers. "I shouldn't have said those things about Eleanor. It wasn't my place to question your new friendship."

"No," I reached across the table to still her nervous hands. "You had every right. We've been friends for a decade. If you can't speak honestly to me, who can?"

Charlie arrived with our order, setting down a pot of tea and two plates bearing blackberry scones.

"Two ladies' specials," he announced. "Freshest batch of the day."

When he'd bustled away, I poured tea for us both, using the familiar ritual to organize my thoughts.

"You were right," I admitted, passing Heidi her cup. "I have been . . . preoccupied with Eleanor lately. And perhaps a bit dismissive of other friendships."

"You've been bewitched by her sophistication." Heidi's tone held no accusation now. Just stating a fact. "I understand the appeal. She's traveled, she's cultured. She makes our little town seem provincial by comparison."

"That's not—" I began, then checked myself. "Well, perhaps that's part of it. But I value your friendship more than any newcomer's, sophisticated or not."

Heidi added a precise teaspoon of sugar to her cup. "I worry about you, Amanda. After finding Mary Alice's body like that . . . it affected you. We all saw it. And then Eleanor swooped in with her calm assurance and worldly wisdom at just the right moment."

I bit into my scone, savoring the tart sweetness that had earned Charlie's baking its reputation throughout the county. "The timing was convenient, wasn't it?"

Heidi's eyes met mine over her teacup. "You've noticed that too?"

I dabbed my lips with a napkin. "And other things. I just came from Ruth Swanson's bookstore. That magazine Eleanor supposedly writes for? It doesn't exist."

Heidi nearly choked on her tea. "What?"

"Ruth checked with every distributor she knows. No one has ever heard of *Angel of the Hearth*. It's entirely fictional." I leaned forward, lowering my voice. "And James has been asking questions about her too. Apparently, there's been a string of fraud cases targeting military families in other towns."

"So I wasn't being petty?" Relief spread across Heidi's face.

"Not petty," I assured her. "Perceptive. I've been so flattered by her attention that I've ignored my instincts—and yours."

The tension between us dissolved like sugar in hot tea. We spent the next half hour catching up on everything we'd missed during our estrangement—choir chitchat, news of Molly's latest letter from Clarence, recipe ideas for the Wheatless Mondays and Meatless Tuesdays the government was calling for.

At last, Heidi checked her pendant watch. "Oh! I need to get back to the shop. Mrs. Davis has been cleaning her closet and promised to drop off some dresses. She has such good taste. If you stop by later, I'll give you first dibs."

We gathered our things, and I insisted on paying Charlie for both of us. While waiting for my change, I noticed the stack of newspapers by the register.

"I'll take one of those too, Charlie." I reached for the Timber Coulee *Gazette.*

Heidi and I stepped outside and embraced.

"Friends again?" I asked.

"Always," she promised as she released me. "And Amanda? Do be careful around Eleanor. Until we know what's really going on."

"I will." I watched as she hurried down the street.

I glanced down at the newspaper in my hand, and its bold headline, "WAR DEPARTMENT WARNS OF FRAUDULENT LETTERS TO SOLDIERS' FAMILIES." My hand trembled as I folded the paper, tucking it under my arm.

"Everything all right, Miss Parrish?" Charlie called from the doorway.

"Fine, thank you." I pasted on a smile. "Just in a hurry to get back to the shop."

As I turned away, I couldn't resist taking a second glance at the paper. My eyes caught on another headline lower on the page. "STERLING CITY AUTHORITIES INVESTIGATING MILITARY PENSION FRAUD." Sterling City—the same place James had mentioned in connection with his investigation.

I quickened my pace toward Mountain Melodies, my mind racing faster than my feet. I had planned to speak with James immediately, but now I had a better idea. Eleanor was staying at the Timber Coulee Hotel. Perhaps it was time I paid her a friendly visit—not to confront her, but to observe more carefully.

If she had been involved in Mary Alice's death, the last thing I wanted was to alert her to my suspicions. But I needed to know more, to confirm what I was beginning to fear.

Surely there was a logical explanation for all of this. It would all be cleared up, and she and I would share a good laugh over it later.

But first, I would visit her. Tomorrow. And I would watch very carefully for any signs that Eleanor Crawford was not the person she claimed to be.

Chapter Eighteen

O n Sunday after church, I balanced the basket of freshly baked cornbread against my hip while reaching for the hotel's brass doorknob. The recipe from my new wartime *Victory Cookbook* had turned out beautifully, and I told myself Eleanor might appreciate a taste of small-town hospitality during her stay at the Timber Coulee Hotel. Besides, I didn't want to return her cookie basket empty.

In reality, though, I was eager to reassure myself that my new friend truly was who she said she was. Although how I was going to accomplish this, I didn't quite know. Steering the conversation toward *Angel of the Hearth* magazine might be a good start.

The lobby's modest chandelier cast warm light across the worn but well-polished floors as I made my way to the front desk.

"Good afternoon, Miss Parrish." Mr. Cavanaugh greeted me with a tip of his head. His family had run the hotel since it opened, and the operation remained a point of local pride. "What brings you by today?"

"I'm visiting Mrs. Crawford." I lifted my basket slightly. "Thought she might enjoy some home baking."

"She's in Room 306." He gestured to the elevator. For all its pretensions of grandeur, our little hotel retained the comfortable, lived-in feeling of a beloved family home.

As I approached Room 306, voices rose from within—an argument in progress. I hesitated, not wanting to intrude on a private moment. Then I caught a fragment that froze me in place.

"—the Wellington woman was getting too close. What choice did I have?" Eleanor's voice, but different somehow—the honeyed Southern accent barely detectable.

"You should have consulted me first." A man's voice, cultured and cool. "Now the sheriff's investigating a murder instead of mere financial discrepancies."

I stood rooted to the spot, the basket heavy in my arms. Murder? Financial discrepancies? Had I stumbled upon a confession?

"That meddling music shop owner might be a problem too," the man continued. "She's entirely too friendly with the sheriff."

"Amanda's harmless," Eleanor replied dismissively. "I've cultivated her trust quite thoroughly. She suspects nothing."

Harmless? Cultivated? The casual dismissal stung.

"And what about Sterling City? That mess nearly exposed the entire operation."

"I've already dealt with the loose ends in Sterling," the man said with chilling finality. "No one connected that widow's accident to our activities."

My heart hammered painfully against my ribs. Sterling City—the very place James had mentioned in connection a widow's "accident" . . . The implications twisted my stomach into knots.

I needed to get out of there. I needed to talk to James.

In my shock, I shifted my weight, causing the floorboard beneath me to emit a betraying creak. The voices inside fell immediately silent.

I quickly rapped on the door, adopting what I hoped was a cheerful expression. "Eleanor? It's Amanda!"

After a moment of tense silence and hurried movements within—drawers closing, papers rustling—the door finally opened. Eleanor stood before me, perfectly composed, her usual warm smile firmly in place.

"Amanda! What a delightful surprise!" The Georgia accent was back in full force, as if it had never disappeared.

"I thought you might enjoy some fresh cornbread." I held up my basket and prayed my face didn't betray what I'd overheard. "I considered making scones, but the government is asking us to use less wheat, so I thought, 'What could I make with corn that would be just as good,' and I landed on cornbread. I hope you like it, even though it's kind of a Southern thing and I'm as Yankee as they come." I heard myself babbling but couldn't seem to stop.

"*Ooh*, I just love a good cornbread. Please, come in." She stepped aside, revealing a well-appointed hotel suite—and a tall, distinguished-looking man standing by the window.

He was handsome in a severe way, with silver-streaked dark hair and a military bearing. Most striking was his resemblance to Eleanor—they shared the same dark eyes and refined features, though his held none of her warmth.

"Amanda, darlin', how sweet of you to stop by. I'd like you to meet w-w-William Crawford," Eleanor said. "My late husband's brother. William, this is Amanda Parrish, the music shop owner I've told you so much about. And my new friend."

"A pleasure." He stepped forward to take my hand. His grip was firm, his smile cool and appraising. "Eleanor speaks very highly of you."

Up close, I detected the distinctive aroma of Turkish cigarettes—clove-scented and expensive, a luxury few in

Timber Coulee could afford. Molly had detected such a unique scent the night she'd interviewed Tommy Morrison at the hotel. This William Crawford must have been the man she'd seen.

"William arrived unexpectedly this mornin'," Eleanor explained. "He's been kind enough to manage Walter's affairs since his passin' and needed my signature on some documents."

"I'm not interrupting anything important, I hope?" I set my basket on the small writing desk, praying I sounded innocent. "Perhaps I should leave." I made a move toward the door, but William's tall frame blocked my exit.

"Not at all," he replied smoothly. "Just some tedious financial matters. Nothing that would interest a creative soul such as yourself."

His condescension was subtle but unmistakable. His eyes swept over me in an assessing manner, as if determining whether I posed any threat. The intensity of his gaze sent a chill down my spine.

"William was just about to leave for a meetin'," Eleanor shot a pointed look at her brother-in-law. "Weren't you, William?"

"Indeed." He checked his pocket watch. "I shouldn't keep Mr. Tate waiting."

"Mr. Tate at the bank?" I said. "But it's Sunday."

"Yes, it's a—a prayer meeting." He collected his hat and coat, nodding politely to me as he passed. "A pleasure to meet you, Miss Parrish. I do hope we'll have the opportunity to become better acquainted on a future visit."

Something in his tone made the words sound more like a threat than a pleasantry. As the door closed behind him, I caught Eleanor watching me with an expression I couldn't quite decipher—calculation, perhaps? Concern? Whatever it was, it vanished quickly beneath her usual sunny demeanor.

"I'm so glad you had an opportunity to meet William." She winked. "He's unattached, you know. Maybe you two should get better acquainted."

An involuntary shudder raised goosebumps on my arms. The last thing I wanted was to spend more time in the presence of those cold black eyes.

"Now, let's see this cornbread you've brought. My, my, it looks yummy." She led me to the small sitting area. "I declare, you Timber Coulee ladies could give our Georgia cooks a run for their money."

As she bustled about near the sink, arranging our impromptu tea with a kettle and a hot plate, I struggled to reconcile the woman before me with the one I'd heard through the door. Which Eleanor was real? The warm, supportive friend, or the cool, calculating woman who considered me "harmless," the one who spoke without a trace of an accent?

Most important, what connection, if any, did she and her brother-in-law have to Mary Alice Wellington? And what had really happened to that widow in Sterling City?

As Eleanor approached with the tea tray, I caught a glimpse of a small brown bottle sitting near the hot plate. Whatever it was, it didn't look like honey. Had she put something in my drink? Or were my suspicions getting the best of me? Too may detective novels, maybe.

Better to be safe than sorry. I rose from my seat. "I'm so sorry, Eleanor. I'd love to stay, but I just remembered something I need to attend to. I'm afraid I must be going."

"Leaving so soon?" She set the tray on the table with a cold smile, her dark eyes glittering. "Why, sugar, you're not going anywhere. Not until we've enjoyed our tea."

Chapter Nineteen

"If you'll excuse me for just a moment." I set down my teacup, unsipped. The small sitting area of Eleanor's hotel suite suddenly felt stifling, as though the walls were closing in around me. "Where might I find the ladies' room?"

"End of the hall to the right, sugar." Eleanor's smile remained fixed and pleasant, but something calculating lingered in her eyes. "Don't be long now. I want to hear all about that ragtime composer you mentioned."

I conjured up what I hoped was a convincing smile. "Of course."

As I stepped into the hallway, I leaned against the wall and drew a deep breath. My mind raced with fragments of the conversation I'd overheard. Mary Alice's murder. Sterling City. A widow's "accident." Each piece connected to the next like a grim puzzle, revealing a picture I could scarcely believe.

The ladies' room was, as Eleanor had said, at the far end of the hallway. I splashed cold water on my face, trying to calm my racing thoughts. I needed to get to James immediately, but first I had to extract myself from Eleanor's company without arousing suspicion. If she truly had been involved somehow in Mary Alice's death . . .

I shuddered at the idea.

After composing myself as best I could, I stepped back into the corridor with one thought.

I had to get out of there. Now.

Later I'd make some apologetic excuse to Eleanor—a sudden and severe bout of indigestion, perhaps, which wasn't so far from the truth. Suspecting her of criminal activity did indeed roil my stomach. But first I'd head straight to the sheriff's office.

As I approached the elevator, I noticed a handwritten sign taped to the brass doors: "Out of Order. Please Use Stairs."

What an annoyance. The elevator had been working perfectly when I arrived less than half an hour ago. Mr. Cavanaugh hadn't mentioned any maintenance scheduled for today.

With a resigned sigh, I turned toward the stairwell door. Three flights down wouldn't take long, and the delay would give me time to compose my thoughts and plan my next move.

The stairwell was dimly lit, with only small windows on each landing allowing the late afternoon sun to filter through. My footsteps echoed against the wooden treads as I began my descent, the sound bouncing off the narrow walls.

I had just reached the first landing when I caught it—the faint but distinctive aroma of clove-scented cigarettes. The same exotic Turkish blend I'd detected on William Crawford.

I froze, suddenly aware I was not alone.

"Hello?" I called, turning to look back up the stairs. "Is someone there?"

Only silence answered me, yet the prickling at the back of my neck intensified. I hastened my steps, eager to reach the lobby and its comforting bustle of activity.

I had descended only a few more steps when I heard it—the soft creak of a floorboard above me. Before I could turn, a sharp push landed between my shoulder blades, propelling me forward with shocking force.

My arms flailed as I pitched headlong down the stairs, my handbag flying from my grasp. For one terrifying moment, I was weightless, suspended in the awful knowledge of what was about to happen.

Then came the impact—my shoulder slamming against the edge of a step, my body tumbling in a painful cascade down the remaining flight. Pain exploded in my arm as it twisted beneath me. My head struck the wall, sending stars bursting across my vision.

I came to rest in a crumpled heap on the lower landing, skirts tangled around my legs, the metallic taste of blood in my mouth where I'd bitten my tongue. Above me, I heard the stairwell door open and close with a soft click.

For several moments, I lay still, fighting waves of nausea and assessing my injuries. My right shoulder throbbed where it had taken the brunt of my fall. My left wrist sent shooting pains up my arm when I attempted to move it. But nothing seemed broken—a small mercy.

With effort, I pushed myself into a sitting position, back against the wall. My scattered belongings lay strewn across the stairs like the aftermath of a storm.

This was no accident. Someone—William Crawford, I had little doubt—had deliberately pushed me down these stairs. The realization raised goosebumps that had nothing to do with the cool air of the stairwell.

I had become a threat to their operation, whatever it was. Just as Mary Alice Wellington had been.

"The Lord is my shepherd," I whispered, drawing strength from the psalm I'd memorized as a child. Fear threatened to overwhelm me, but faith pushed back against it. If God had preserved me through this accident, perhaps He still had work for me to do.

If Mary Alice could face danger in pursuit of justice, so could I.

The door below me opened, and I tensed, ready to defend myself if my attacker had returned to finish what he'd started. Instead, young Tommy Morrison, one of the hotel's bellhops, appeared, his freckled face registering shock when he saw me.

"Miss Parrish! Are you hurt?" He bounded up the stairs toward me. "What happened?"

"I fell," I said simply, not ready to share my suspicions. "The steps must have been more slippery than I realized."

"Let me help you, ma'am. Should I call for Dr. Moriarty?"

"No, that won't be necessary." I winced as he helped me to my feet. "If you could just help me gather my things and assist me to the lobby . . ."

My arm protested sharply when I moved it, confirming my suspicion of a sprain. Tommy collected my scattered belongings with the eager efficiency of youth.

As we made our painful progress down the remaining flight of stairs, my emotions spiraled. I needed to reach James, to tell him everything—the conversation I'd overheard, my suspicions about Eleanor and William, the connection to Sterling City.

But first, I would have to face Eleanor herself.

She was waiting in the lobby, apparently having grown concerned at my long absence. Her expression shifted from impatience to perfect shock and concern when she saw me limping on Tommy's arm, my hair coming loose from its pins, a bruise no doubt already forming on my cheekbone.

"Amanda! Sweet heaven, what happened?" She rushed forward, her Georgia accent in full bloom, her face a mask of distress so convincing I might have believed it had I not overheard her earlier conversation.

"She had a fall in the stairwell, ma'am," Tommy explained.

"Oh, you poor thing!" Eleanor's arm slipped around my waist, taking over from Tommy with seemingly genuine concern. "What were you doin' in the stairwell? I thought you were just goin' to the ladies' room."

"I did. But then . . ." For the life of me, I couldn't think up a plausible excuse for running out on her. Fortunately she didn't pursue that particular line of questioning.

"Well, for heaven's sake, next time take the elevator."

"It was out of order." I winced as I clutched my elbow. "There was a sign."

"Was there? How odd." Her brow creased in what appeared to be honest confusion.

Mr. Cavanaugh, who had been helping another guest at the front desk, hurried over with a frown. "What's this about the elevator being out of order? Nobody informed me of any problems today."

"There was a sign on the door," I explained, my cheeks warming with embarrassment at being the center of attention. "A handwritten one."

Mr. Cavanaugh's face darkened. "Tommy, check the elevator immediately. And find that sign."

"Yes, sir!" The bellhop dashed off, returning moments later slightly out of breath. "The elevator's working fine, sir. And there's no sign now."

My palms turned clammy as the implication became clear. The sign had been placed deliberately to divert me to the stairs—where my attacker had been waiting. And I didn't need three guesses to know who the attacker was.

"How very peculiar," Eleanor murmured, her arm still supporting me. "Amanda, you're trembling. Let's get you seated and have some tea brought over."

No! No tea. Summoning as much composure as I could, I said, "I should be getting home. Molly will be wondering where I am."

"Nonsense. You can't possibly walk home in this condition." Eleanor's tone brooked no argument. "Mr. Cavanaugh, would you be kind enough to send someone for Sheriff Holcomb? I believe he should know about this incident."

I glanced at her sharply, searching for any hint of calculation behind her concern. Was she truly worried for my safety, or merely ensuring she appeared appropriately solicitous in front of witnesses?

"That won't be necessary," I said, but Mr. Cavanaugh was already dispatching Tommy on the errand.

"The sheriff will want to investigate," Eleanor insisted. "An accident like this , , , it's most irregular."

She guided me to a chair in the lobby, her hand gripping mine with what seemed like true concern. Was this all part of a performance? And if so, what role was I playing in their scheme?

One thing was certain—when James arrived, I would need to get him alone. There was too much at stake to remain silent, no matter how convincing Eleanor's act of friendship might be.

The game had changed, and I was now a player whether I wished to be or not.

Chapter Twenty

The hotel lobby had transformed into an impromptu investigation scene. Mr. Cavanaugh had ushered other guests away and drawn the curtains against curious onlookers from the street. My wrist, now properly wrapped and cushioned by a pillow, throbbed with each heartbeat.

Eleanor hadn't left my side since my fall, maintaining a constant stream of concerned chatter while ordering tea, cold compresses, and a telephone call to Dr. Moriarty, who fortunately was making house calls on the other side of town. Her solicitousness felt smothering, especially as I desperately needed a private word with James.

The hotel's front door swung open, and James Holcomb strode in, his tall frame filling the doorway. His sheriff's badge caught the afternoon light, but it was the concern etched on his face that made my heart skip.

"Amanda." He crossed the lobby in four long strides, taking in my disheveled appearance with a quick, assessing glance. His hand hovered near my shoulder before dropping back to his side—always careful to maintain a proper distance between us in public. "What happened?"

Before I could answer, Eleanor jumped in. "She took a terrible fall down the stairs, Sheriff. The poor dear could have broken her neck!" Her Southern accent seemed to intensify in James's presence. "Someone had put up a sign claimin' the elevator was out of order, but when Tommy checked afterward, there was no sign and the elevator was workin' perfectly."

James's eyes narrowed. "Is that so?" He turned to Mr. Cavanaugh. "Any idea who might have posted such a sign?"

"None, Sheriff. I've questioned the staff, and nobody admits to having seen it before Miss Parrish mentioned it." The hotel manager twisted his hands nervously. "Beyond the occasional harmless prankster, we've never had an incident like this before."

James's expression remained neutral but his eyes missed nothing. "I'd like to see the stairwell where this occurred."

"Of course," Mr. Cavanaugh said. "Right this way."

"A moment, if I may." James turned back to me. "Amanda, are you able to show me exactly where you fell?"

"Yes, sir," I replied, seizing the opportunity to speak to him in private.

"I'll help her," Eleanor offered immediately, reaching for uninjured arm.

"That's kind of you, Mrs. Crawford," James replied, his tone professionally courteous, "but I'd like to speak with Miss Parrish alone about what she experienced. Standard procedure."

A flicker of something—annoyance? concern?—crossed Eleanor's features before her pleasant smile returned. "Of course, Sheriff. I understand completely." She squeezed my hand. "I'll just wait here, sugar."

James offered his arm, and I leaned on him gratefully as we made our way to the stairwell. Mr. Cavanaugh opened the door for us, then discreetly stepped back into the lobby at James's nod.

The moment the door closed behind us, James's professional demeanor softened. "Are you truly all right?" His voice roughened with concern. "That bruise looks painful."

"I've had worse." Though in truth, every movement sent jolts of pain through my wrist and shoulder. "James, I need to tell you something, and we don't have much time."

His expression sobered. "What is it?"

"When I arrived at the hotel today, I overheard a conversation between Eleanor and a man she later introduced as William Crawford, her brother-in-law." The words tumbled out in an urgent whisper as we slowly ascended to the landing where I'd fallen. "They were discussing something about a 'soldier's widow' and mentioned Sterling City."

James went very still, his arm tightening almost imperceptibly around my waist. "You're certain?"

"Absolutely. I couldn't hear everything clearly, but they fell silent when they realized I was there. And there was something . . . off about the way she introduced him."

"In what way?"

"It felt rehearsed." I indicated the landing where I'd come to rest after my fall. "This is where I ended up. And James, I didn't simply fall. I felt a push between my shoulder blades. I'm certain of it."

He studied the stairwell with a professional eye, noting the height of the railings, the steep angle of the steps, the limited lighting. "Did you see who pushed you?"

"No, but I smelled something distinctive—Turkish cigarettes with a clove scent. The same aroma I noticed on William Crawford earlier." I paused to breathe. "And the fake sign on the elevator . . . what if it was deliberate, to ensure I'd use the stairs?"

James surveyed the landing carefully. "This would be a difficult case to prove, Amanda. Without witnesses or evidence beyond the missing sign . . ."

"You don't believe me?" Disappointment stabbed me deep inside.

"I didn't say that." His voice was gentle but firm. "I believe you experienced what you're describing. But proving malicious intent would be challenging. Mr. Cavanaugh says practical jokes involving fake 'out of order' signs have happened before."

"This was no practical joke," I insisted.

"I know." He spoke so quietly I nearly missed it. "But officially, this will have to be recorded as an accident until we have more evidence."

"More evidence of what, exactly?" I pressed. "You suspect them too, don't you?"

James sighed, running a hand through his hair—a gesture I recognized from our years of friendship. It meant he was wrestling with something he couldn't yet share.

"I'm waiting for a response from the War Department about Walter Crawford's service record."

"What about Eleanor's journalism career? The magazine she claims to write for doesn't exist—Ruth Swanson confirmed it."

"That's not necessarily evidence of criminal activity," James pointed out. "People fabricate credentials for many reasons. Some harmless, some not."

I could tell he was holding back, maintaining his professional reserve. "There's more, isn't there? Something you're not telling me."

"There are aspects of this investigation I can't discuss yet, even with you." His expression softened. "Especially with you, Amanda. The less you appear to know, the safer you'll be."

The implication made my heart plummet. "You think I'm in danger."

"I think," he said with deliberate care, "that falling down stairs is rarely an innocent accident when it happens to someone who's been asking questions."

The stairwell door below us opened, and Eleanor's voice floated up. "Amanda? Sheriff? Is everything all right up there?"

James and I exchanged a quick glance.

"Just examining the scene," James called down slipping effortlessly back into his official persona. "We'll be with you momentarily."

He turned to me, his voice dropping to a whisper. "For now, we treat this as an unfortunate accident. I'll file the report accordingly. But I want you to keep your distance from both Eleanor and her brother-in-law until I've completed my inquiries."

"But what about the choir? Tomorrow's Monday. We have a rehearsal, then the dress rehearsal on Wednesday and the concert on Thursday—Memorial Day."

"Attend as normal. Don't give them any reason to suspect you're wary of them." He paused. "I'm going to visit the Thornton family on Tuesday. That letter about their son troubles me. Would you be willing to accompany me? Viola might be more forthcoming with you present."

"Of course" The request surprised me, but I was pleased to be included.

"Good. I'll collect you Tuesday at seven." He helped me back down the stairs, his steady presence reassuring despite the uncertainty of the situation.

At the doorway, Eleanor waited, her face a perfect mask of concern.

"There you are! I was getting worried." She moved to take my other arm. "What did you discover, Sheriff?"

"Nothing conclusive." James's tone remained professionally neutral. "Just an unfortunate accident. These stairwells can be treacherous, especially with their dim lighting."

"But what about the sign?" Eleanor asked. "Surely someone playin' such a dangerous prank should be held accountable?"

"We'll continue looking into it," James assured her. "For now, Miss Parrish should rest that wrist. I can drive her home if you'd like."

"That's not necessary," Eleanor insisted. "I'd be happy to accompany Amanda home myself. William has offered his automobile."

James tensed slightly beside me. "That's very kind, Mrs. Crawford, but I'd prefer to handle it myself. I need to ask Miss Parrish a few more questions about what she observed before her fall."

Eleanor's smile dimmed only slightly. "Of course, Sheriff. I wouldn't dream of interferin' with official business." She squeezed my hand. "I'll stop by this evenin' to check on you, sugar. Perhaps bring some of that liniment my grandmother swore by for sprains."

"Thank you." I plastered on a smile of false gratitude. "You're too kind."

As James guided me to his waiting automobile, I glanced back to see Eleanor watching from the hotel entrance. Something in her stance—the careful stillness, the watchful eyes—reminded me of a predator assessing potential prey. Our eyes met briefly, and though her expression remained pleasant, I felt scrutinized. Her gaze flicked to James's badge before shifting back to me.

"That woman," James murmured as he helped me into the passenger seat, "is trouble."

Chapter Twenty-One

"Aunt Amanda!" Molly swung open the screen door at our approach, her face paling at the sight of my bruised cheek and bandaged arm. "What on earth happened?"

"A fall at the hotel." I kept the explanation simple. "Nothing broken, just a bit battered."

"A nasty fall down a staircase." James helped me to the sofa where Moxie immediately jumped up to investigate my injuries with suspicious sniffs. "Keep your doors locked."

Molly's eyes widened. "Lock our doors? But why would—"

"Just a precaution," I interrupted, not wanting to worry her unnecessarily. "Thank you, James. We'll be waiting for news."

After the sheriff left, Molly brought tea and demanded a full account of my "accident." I gave her an edited version, omitting the conversation I'd overheard and my suspicions about Eleanor and William. The less she knew, the safer she would be.

"It all sounds very odd." Molly frowned as she refilled my teacup. "A sign that disappeared, a mysterious fall . . . and why would Sheriff Holcomb tell us to lock our doors over a simple accident?"

Before I could formulate a suitably reassuring response, a sharp knock at the door made us both start. Moxie's fur bristled as he leapt from my lap to the windowsill, tail twitching.

Molly peered through the curtains. "It's only Eleanor. And she's brought someone with her." She took a second look. "I think it might be the man I saw asking about her at the hotel."

My senses went on alert. "William Crawford," I murmured.

"You know him?" Molly stared at me, eyes round.

"We were introduced today. He's Eleanor's brother-in-law." I grasped Molly's hand as she moved toward the door. "Don't let them in, Molly. Tell them I'm resting and can't be disturbed."

She stared at me, confusion evident in her expression. "But Eleanor's been such a good friend to you. And she's come all this way—"

"Please, Molly." I tightened my grip on her hand. "Trust me on this. I'll explain everything later, but for now, please just send them away."

Perhaps it was the urgency in my voice, or the fear I couldn't quite conceal, but Molly simply nodded and stepped outside to the porch, pulling the door closed behind her. I heard the murmur of voices, Eleanor's sweet tones rising in apparent concern, then William's deeper response. Finally, their footsteps descended the porch steps and faded away.

Molly returned, her expression troubled. "They've gone, but Eleanor seemed hurt. She left some kind of liniment she said would help with the pain." She placed a small jar on the side table. "What's really going on? You've never turned anyone away before."

I sighed, knowing I owed her some explanation. "It's complicated, Molly. I've learned some . . . disturbing things today. Things that suggest Eleanor may not be who she claims to be."

Then I told her everything I knew. We sat and talked, deep into the night. And from Molly's wise and heartfelt responses, I realized I didn't need Eleanor, after all. I had a best friend already, right here, sitting on my sofa.

Chapter Twenty-Two

The Thorntons' house was a modest two-story structure on Maple Street, with crisp white clapboard siding and emerald-green shutters. A pair of fragrant lilacs flanked the walkway, their cheerful purple blooms at odds with the solemn purpose of our visit.

James had asked me to accompany him, feeling my presence might make things easier for the family—particularly Viola, who had been withdrawn and anxious since Mary Alice's murder. My concern for the young woman kept me engaged with the investigation, even though it appeared Molly's name had been cleared. Tommy Morrison had corroborated her story about her whereabouts at the time of the murder.

Mrs. Thornton answered our knock, her face tight with apprehension when she saw the sheriff standing on her porch. "Sheriff Holcomb, Miss Parrish." She smoothed her apron with nervous hands. "Please, come in. My husband is in the parlor." She peered at my bruised face.

"Just a clumsy fall," I assured her before she could ask. "It looks worse than it is."

She led us through a narrow hallway into a tidy parlor where Mr. Thornton sat in an armchair, a newspaper folded across his knee. He rose when we entered, his expression wary.

"Sheriff." He extended his hand. "Have you news of Edward?"

"In a manner of speaking." James shook the offered hand. "Is your daughter at home? I'd like her to be present for this conversation as well."

A shadow crossed Mrs. Thornton's face. "She's upstairs. She's mostly kept to herself since . . ." she trailed off, glancing at me.

"I understand," I said. "Would you like me to go up to her?"

Mrs. Thornton gave a grateful nod. "Second door on the right. She's been so troubled lately. Perhaps you can convince her to come down."

I climbed the narrow staircase, my footsteps muffled by the braided runner that covered the wooden steps. At Viola's door, I knocked softly.

"Viola? It's Amanda Parrish. May I come in?"

A faint sound from within might have been assent. I turned the knob and entered a neat bedroom with floral wallpaper and a small writing desk positioned beneath the window. Viola sat on the edge of her bed, a piece of paper clutched in her hand, her eyes red from crying.

"Sheriff Holcomb is downstairs." I sat beside her. "He has information about the letter your family received regarding Edward."

Her head jerked up, eyes wide with fear. "What kind of information?"

"I think it would be best if you came down to hear it directly from him."

She clutched the paper more tightly, her knuckles whitening.

"Viola, is something wrong? Beyond worry for your brother, I mean."

She looked away, her bottom lip trembling. "I can't," she whispered.

"Can't what?"

"Can't face them. Not after what I've done." A tear slipped down her cheek.

I laid my hand over hers, her trembling fingers beneath mine. "Whatever it is, Viola, facing it is the first step toward making it right."

She drew a shaky breath, then stood, squaring her shoulders with visible effort. "You're right. I need to tell the truth. All of it." She folded the piece of paper and slipped it into her skirt pocket.

Downstairs, James had arranged himself in a straight-backed chair opposite the Thorntons, who sat side by side on their sofa. He rose when Viola entered, giving her a gentle nod.

"Thank you for joining us, Miss Thornton." He used his formal sheriff voice. "Please, have a seat."

Viola perched on the edge of an ottoman, her posture rigid.

I sat beside her, offering silent support.

James withdrew the letter from his inside pocket and unfolded it. "Mr. and Mrs. Thornton, I've completed my investigation of this letter about your son. I need to inform you that it's fraudulent—a forgery designed to extort money from your family."

Mrs. Thornton gasped, pressing a hand to her chest. "Fraudulent? But it looks so official!"

"That's precisely what makes these schemes so dangerous," James explained. "They prey on families' natural concern for their loved ones serving overseas."

"Are you quite certain?" Mr. Thornton leaned forward to examine the letter James held. "It bears the official letterhead and everything."

"I've confirmed with military authorities," James said. "There is no Captain Joseph Harris at Fort Leavenworth. Furthermore, the military doesn't address gambling debts through family members—any such issues would be handled through the soldier's chain of command."

"Then Edward isn't in trouble?" Hope lighted Mrs. Thornton's features.

"No, ma'am. In fact, I received a telegram this morning confirming that Private Thornton is serving honorably with his unit. He is not under any disciplinary action."

Mrs. Thornton began to weep with relief, while Mr. Thornton sat back heavily, running a hand over his face.

"Thank God," he murmured. "We were about to mortgage the house. We'd already spoken to the bank."

"I know who sent it," Viola said suddenly, her voice barely above a whisper.

Four pairs of eyes turned to her in surprise, including mine.

"Viola?" her father said. "What are you talking about?"

"I didn't know it was fraud." Her voice quavered. "I thought I was helping Edward."

"Miss Thornton," James said, "do you have information about who sent this letter to your parents?"

Viola sniffled. "Mrs. Crawford. Eleanor Crawford. She told me she had connections in the War Department who could help Edward get transferred to a safer position. All I had to do was help her gather some information."

"Information?" James prompted when she faltered.

"About families in town with sons or husbands serving overseas. Who received allotments, who had life insurance policies, which units they served with." Viola's shoulders slumped with shame. "She said it was for an article she was writing about supporting our troops. I believed her."

I could scarcely believe what I was hearing, but James's expression remained unchanged. "Where did you obtain this information?"

After wiping her face with a handkerchief offered by her father, Viola said in a tiny voice, "From Mr. and Mrs. Talbott."

"Your employers at the Hummingbird Tearoom?" Her mother was aghast. "How are they involved in this?"

"They both volunteer with the Red Cross. And sometimes they bring paperwork to the tearoom."

"And they shared this information with you?"

"No, not exactly." Viola twisted the handkerchief. "They didn't know. I copied things from the paperwork when they weren't looking. Things Mrs. Crawford asked for."

Mrs. Thornton stared at her daughter in shocked disbelief. "Viola, what have you done?"

"I didn't know what she was up to!" Viola cried. "I trusted her. She was so kind, so interested in Edward. She said she understood what it was like to worry about someone overseas because her husband had died in the war."

"And she asked about Edward?"

"Yes. She seemed genuinely concerned. Then a few days later, she mentioned her War Department connections. Said she could help ensure Edward's safety." Viola reached into her skirt pocket, pulled out the piece of paper, and unfolded it. It appeared to be a note of some kind. "Then this came. She told me not to mention our arrangement to anyone, that her contacts needed to stay confidential."

She held out the note to James. "She wanted me to get my parents' bank information. For the transfer that would help Edward."

James scanned the note, his expression darkening. "This is part of the same scheme, Miss Thornton. I'm afraid you've been manipulated."

Mr. Thornton's face had flushed deep red with anger. "How could you be so foolish, Viola? Giving out private family information to a stranger?"

"I was trying to help Edward!" Viola sobbed. "I was so worried about him!"

"We all were," Mrs. Thornton murmured. "But this—"

"Eleanor Crawford took advantage of your daughter's concern for her brother," I interrupted gently. "She's done the same to other families in other towns. Viola isn't the first to be deceived by her."

"Miss Parrish is right," James added. "These charlatans are skilled at manipulating fears and hopes. They know exactly which emotional strings to pull."

"I haven't given her the bank information. Not yet. But I'm afraid of what she'll do to me when I don't come through." Viola looked up at me with red-rimmed eyes. "Is that why Mrs. Wellington was killed? Because she found out what Mrs. Crawford was doing?"

A heavy silence fell over the room. James adjusted his position, clearly weighing how much to share with the family.

"We have reason to believe Mrs. Wellington discovered evidence of financial irregularities connected to the Ladies' Aid Society," he said. "Whether that's connected to her death is still under investigation."

"Oh, no," Viola whispered, her face crumpling. "I've ruined everything. If I hadn't helped her—"

"This is not your fault," I stated, taking her cold hands in mine. "You were trying to protect your brother. Eleanor Crawford is the one who exploited that love for her own purposes."

James nodded in agreement. "Miss Thornton, I'm going to need a full statement from you about your interactions with Eleanor Crawford. Every detail could be important."

Viola straightened, mopping her face with the handkerchief. "Of course. I'll tell you everything I know."

"I'd like to keep this note Eleanor sent to Viola." He folded it and placed it in his breast pocket. "It could be important to our investigation."

"Take it," Viola said. "Take anything that helps you catch her."

James rose. "I'll need you to come to my office tomorrow morning to make your formal statement, Miss Thornton. Around ten o'clock?"

"I'll be there," she promised.

As we prepared to leave, Mr. Thornton caught James by the arm. "Sheriff, what would have happened if we'd sent that money? Would we ever have seen it again?"

"No, sir," James replied honestly. "These imposters move quickly. Once the money is wired, they withdraw it immediately and disappear. They're usually long gone before families realize they've been deceived."

Mr. Thornton's expression hardened. "Find her, Sheriff. Find her and make her pay for what she's done."

"I intend to, Mr. Thornton," James said gravely. "You have my word on that."

Outside, the afternoon had grown chilly, gray clouds gathering on the horizon. James and I walked in silence until we reached the corner of Maple and Elm.

"What happens now?" I asked.

"Now we have direct evidence connecting Eleanor to the fraud scheme." James patted his pocket where Viola's letter rested. "But we still need more to tie her conclusively to Mary Alice's murder."

"Do you believe what Viola said? That Mary Alice might have been killed because she discovered what Eleanor was doing?"

James nodded. "It fits. Mary Alice was meticulous about finances. If she noticed discrepancies in the Ladies' Aid accounts, she would have investigated. And if she confronted Eleanor . . ."

He didn't need to finish the thought. We both knew what might have happened next.

"Do take care around Eleanor," James cautioned as we said good-night at my front door. "Now that we know what she's capable of, she's more dangerous than ever."

"I will." A sense of foreboding ran through me at the thought of facing her at tomorrow's choir rehearsal, pretending I knew nothing of her deceptions.

As James walked toward his office, his shoulders squared with resolve, I felt a strange mixture of dread and determination. The pieces were coming together now, forming a picture of calculation and cruelty that had cost Mary Alice her life.

Eleanor Crawford wasn't just a fraud. She was a killer. And somehow, we needed to prove it before she claimed another victim.

On Wednesday morning, Mrs. Henderson sorted through a stack of Beethoven sonatas on the counter, her lips pursed in concentration. "I'm not sure which would be appropriate for my Gertie. She's quite talented, you know, but still only twelve."

"The Sonatina in G Major might be a good starting point." I pulled the sheet music from a display behind me. "It's not too difficult but still challenges—"

A loud, plaintive yowl from the stockroom caused us both to jump. I cast an apologetic smile at Mrs. Henderson, who raised an eyebrow.

"My cat," I explained. "He must have gotten himself shut in again."

Another yowl, this one longer and more insistent. Mrs. Henderson's eyebrow climbed higher than I would have thought possible.

"The poor creature sounds distressed," she observed. "Perhaps you should check on him?"

"Moxie is a master of melodrama," Molly called down from her perch high on a ladder, where she was polishing the woodwind instruments. "Last week he made the same fuss over a spider in his water dish."

I returned my attention to the music selection, but Moxie was not to be ignored. His third yowl contained a series of staccato notes suggestive of a Wagner aria.

"I've never heard a cat make quite that sound," Mrs. Henderson said.

"He's . . . unusually expressive." My voice was weak with embarrassment.

While Mrs. Henderson continued browsing, I moved to the stockroom door and swished the curtain open just enough to hiss, "Moxie! Pipe down!"

A streak of orange fur shot between my ankles, nearly tripping me. Moxie raced to the counter, jumped up beside the startled Mrs. Henderson, and proceeded to meow directly into her face.

"Well!" she exclaimed, jerking backward. "What an enthusiastic animal."

"I'm so sorry." My mortification knew no bounds. "He's not usually this rude to customers."

"Perhaps he's trying to sell me something," Mrs. Henderson remarked in a dry tone. "Yodeling lessons, perhaps?"

I gave a nervous laugh and tried to scoop up the cat, who dodged my grasp and jumped back to the floor. He ran back to the stockroom door, yowling and looking over his shoulder at me.

"I think he wants you to follow him," Mrs. Henderson observed. "Like in those moving picture shows where the dog leads people to the child who's fallen down a well."

"Moxie is certainly dramatic enough for the cinema." I watched him with a wary eye. "But I assure you, there are no wells in my stockroom."

Mrs. Henderson gathered up the Beethoven sonatina and a book of Bach preludes. "I'll take these for now. You'd better see what's agitating your little performer before he disturbs your other customers."

I glanced around the empty shop. "You're very kind. Let me ring these up for you."

As I wrapped her purchases, Moxie continued his performance, darting between the stockroom door and my ankles, occasionally batting at my skirt with his paw.

"Do let me know what catastrophe he's discovered." Mrs. Henderson gathered her package. "I haven't been this curious since Reverend Miller's toupee blew off during the Easter service."

I managed a strained smile. "I'm sure it's nothing nearly so exciting."

The moment Mrs. Henderson left, I wobbled toward the stockroom, Moxie weaving frantically between my feet. "This had better be important," I warned him.

Moxie dashed ahead of me into the room. I followed, looking first at his water dish, then at his favorite napping spot atop a stack of shipping crates. Nothing seemed amiss.

"Well?" I demanded. "What's all the fuss about?"

He jumped to a high shelf and yowled.

Then I saw it, and I slapped my hand over my mouth.

"Oh, no! Not again!"

Chapter Twenty-Three

"Molly! Come quickly!"

I stood in the doorway of the storage room, staring in dismay at the growing puddle seeping across the floor, directly beneath a dark stain spreading on the ceiling. Water dripped steadily onto a stack of choir music folders we'd placed on a shelf after Monday's rehearsal.

Molly appeared behind me, her gasp turning into a groan as she took in the scene. "Not again!"

I grabbed a metal wastebasket and positioned it to catch the worst of the dripping. "Start moving those folders before they're completely ruined." The last burst pipe had ruined the shop's piano. At least this time it was only damaging paper, not an expensive instrument.

We worked quickly, salvaging what we could. The top folders were already soaked through, the ink bleeding on several pages of carefully arranged musical scores.

"This is a disaster," Molly muttered, spreading wet pages across every available surface. "Judith will be beside herself. The concert's tomorrow, and we're supposed to bring all these folders to dress rehearsal tonight."

I sighed, eyeing the spreading water stain on the ceiling. "I'll telephone Mr. Drummond. Though heaven knows how long it will take him to get here."

"If only Ernie were still around," Molly said softly.

My heart gave a familiar twinge at the mention of Ernie Wendell. The old handyman had been a fixture in Timber Coulee for decades—and my dear friend—before his murder two summers ago. That case had been solved, but the hole left by Ernie's absence remained unfilled.

"Ernie would have fixed that pipe properly the first time." How I missed his methodical approach to any repair. "He wouldn't have left it vulnerable to more leaks."

"And he'd be here in ten minutes flat, toolbox in hand."

I smiled in spite of myself. "With a thermos of coffee and probably some outlandish story about the time he fixed a similar leak at the governor's mansion."

"Were his stories true?" Molly carefully separated sodden sheets and spread them on shelves and the floor.

"About half of them, I'd guess. Though Sarah always believed every word." The memory of Sarah's delighted laughter at Ernie's tall tales surfaced unexpectedly. "She'd pretend to be skeptical, but she loved his stories. Said they were good for the soul."

Molly gave me a sympathetic glance. "You've lost a lot of people you care about."

"Yes." I swallowed the sudden lump in my throat. "Too many."

I turned away, ostensibly to check the spreading stain but really to compose myself. The grief came in waves still—less frequent now, but no less intense when they hit. Sarah, Ernie . . . even Mary Alice Wellington, though I'd never have counted her among those I cared for.

"It's strange." I turned back to Molly. "I didn't even like Mary Alice very much. Few people did. But I can't stop thinking about her lying there, about who would do such a thing."

"Because it happened in your shop?"

"Partly. But also because . . ." I searched for the words. "Everyone deserves justice, Molly. Even difficult people like Mary Alice."

Molly nodded, understanding in her eyes. "Maybe especially them, since they have fewer people fighting for them."

I squeezed her shoulder. "I'm going to call Mr. Drummond. Keep separating those pages—if we can dry them quickly, maybe they won't be completely ruined."

I made my way to the telephone, mentally preparing for Mr. Drummond's excuses and delays. As I waited for the operator, I glanced back at Molly meticulously spreading music sheets across the counter, chairs, and even the floor.

Mary Alice Wellington may have been the most demanding, critical member of our choir, but she deserved better than to be strangled in my shop, her death used to cast suspicion on innocent people. Someone had deliberately created this vicious scenario, and I was determined to find out who.

As the operator connecting me with Mr. Drummond's house and his wife came on the line, I returned my attention to the immediate crisis. First the leak, then the murder. One problem at a time.

An hour later, I'd received Mr. Drummond's promise to come "first thing tomorrow" and had placed every pot and bucket we owned under strategic drips. I set up an electric fan to encourage the paper to dry faster, but first had to secure each piece under makeshift paperweights to keep them from fluttering into chaos. Molly remained focused on salvaging the music, now working her way through Mary Alice's folder—recognizable by the neat label in Mary Alice's handwriting.

"Aunt Amanda?" Molly's voice held an odd note that immediately caught my attention.

"What is it?" I approached where she knelt amid a sea of drying paper.

"I found something." She handed me a manila envelope. "It was at the very back of Mary Alice's folder."

The envelope was plain, unremarkable, the kind sold at Henderson's General Store for a nickel. Mercifully, it had escaped water damage.

"Look inside," Molly urged, her eyes wide.

Inside, in Mary Alice's precise handwriting, were notes about several Timber Coulee families with men serving overseas—details about allotments, benefits, and financial arrangements. But, more important, there were observations about unusual letters, unexpected financial difficulties, and questions about official communications.

Next was a page marked "L. A. S. Discrepancies." Mary Alice had documented several unexplained withdrawals from the society's account over the past months, along with notes about who had access to the funds.

Behind that page was another titled "Suspicious Correspondence." Mary Alice had documented several instances of families receiving unusual letters about their loved ones—including the Thorntons' letter about Edward's gambling debts.

"Everyone was blaming her for the shortfall," Molly said.

"This looks like some kind of investigation." My eyes skimmed her meticulous notes.

"That's what I thought." Molly leaned closer. "Look at the last few pages."

I turned to find a series of letters—correspondence between Mary Alice and the officers of Ladies' Aid societies in other towns. In each, she inquired about a woman matching Eleanor's description, though under different names, Nora Campbell in Portland, Ella Winters in Sterling City.

The replies confirmed her suspicions. Each society had experienced financial irregularities during the woman's tenure, and each time she had departed suddenly for a "family emergency" or other matter of some urgency.

The final letter was a carbon copy of a letter addressed to the War Department's fraud investigation unit. I read the second paragraph aloud.

"'I have uncovered what appears to be a systematic scheme to defraud military families through the Ladies' Aid Society and possibly other organizations, like the Red Cross. Funds designated for war relief are being diverted, and several families have received falsified communications regarding their loved ones overseas, requesting money for various fictitious emergencies. Most troubling is the possibility that this scheme extends beyond our small community.'" The letter was signed "M. A. Wellington, Treasurer, Ladies' Aid Society, Timber Coulee, Idaho."

Molly and I looked at each other in silence for a moment. Then I said, "So Mary Alice wasn't just being nosy about military families. She was investigating fraud."

"It appears so," Molly concurred. "Which maybe means her remarks weren't meant to belittle anyone's service."

"She was trying to protect them," I whispered, shame washing over me as I remembered how quickly I'd judged her. "And someone silenced her for it."

There was a handwritten note on the bottom of the carbon copy. Mary Alice's usually neat script was hurried, anxious.

E. C. (alias E. Winters, N. Campbell?) asking pointed questions about allotments again. Watched her copy addresses from Ladies' Aid records when she thought no one was looking. Pattern matches other societies' reports. Missing funds coincide with her arrival dates. Need more proof before taking to authorities. Must speak with M. A. —glad for her assistance.

"E. C.? M. A.?" Molly's brow creased.

"Eleanor Crawford. Mildred Abernathy." My hand trembled as I placed the papers back into the envelope. "She deduced it," I whispered. "Mary Alice determined Eleanor was behind the missing funds—and something more."

"I think she suspected Eleanor of running some kind of scheme targeting soldiers' families." Molly blurted. "And that's why she was asking all those questions about military service and payments during rehearsal. And it sounds like Mildred Abernathy might have been helping with the investigation."

"And look here." From the very back of the folder, I pulled out a newspaper clipping—a photo—with an alarming handwritten note in the margin. Looking over my shoulder, Molly gasped.

What we'd all interpreted as Mary Alice's unpatriotic nosiness had actually been her attempt to identify vulnerable families—families that might be targeted by an imposter.

And now it appeared we had proof.

Chapter Twenty-Four

The rain had finally stopped, leaving behind puddles that reflected the evening sky in muted shades of purple and gray. I stood at the window of Mountain Melodies as James crossed the street toward my shop. His expression was grim, his shoulders set with determination.

I had telephoned his office an hour earlier, asking him to come alone. "I've found something," was all I'd said. He hadn't asked questions—just promised to be there by six.

The door creaked under the muffled bell as he entered, water still dripping from his coat.

"Amanda." He nodded formally, removing his hat. "You said it was important."

"It is." I moved to the counter where I'd arranged my evidence in careful piles. "I think I know who killed Mary Alice."

His expression remained neutral, professional. "I'm listening."

I took a deep breath. "First, I need to know something. Did your telegrams to other towns turn up anything? Anything unusual?"

James hesitated, then relented. "Yes. In three previous towns, a pattern has been established of extortion letters received by military families and discrepancies turning up in the financial accounts of charitable organizations. The cases haven't been solved yet, though."

"So someone—or someones, plural—is traveling around, committing fraud?"

"That is my initial suspicion, but—" He stopped himself. "Amanda, I can't discuss all the details of an ongoing investigation with a civilian."

"Even if that civilian has evidence that might solve the crime?" I spread several papers across the counter. "I've been doing some investigating of my own."

His jaw tightened. "I asked you not to interfere."

"And I ignored you. Are you going to hear me out, or shall I take this to the state police instead?"

The threat was hollow—we both knew it—but something in my tone must have convinced him I was serious. He sighed, setting his hat on the counter.

"What have you found?"

"Remember this article about the war widow fraud in Sterling City?"

"I've seen it," James acknowledged.

"Then you know the fraud involved someone gathering detailed information about soldiers' families, then using that information to forge documents and claim benefits. Someone who would need to know exactly which families had loved ones overseas, what units they served in, and what their financial arrangements were."

Light flickered in his eyes. "The same kind of information Mary Alice was collecting."

I nodded. "But she wasn't the one running the fraud scheme, James. She was investigating it."

I pushed forward the manila envelope. "This was hidden in Mary Alice's music folder. Molly found it while drying out the choir music after another leaking-pipe fiasco."

James opened it and leafed through the papers.

"She suspected someone was targeting our soldiers' families," I continued. "Specifically, she was concerned about the Thornton family, about that letter claiming Edward was in trouble for gambling debts and needed money wired immediately. And remember Beatrice Fairmont's concerns about her Henry's supposed debts."

"That also fits a new development. Just this morning Rose MacTavish brought me a letter that supposedly came from the British military concerning money owed by her husband, Callan. But she immediately knew it was a fraud and brought it straight to me."

"Rose is very sharp," I said. "But the nerve of those criminals. British military, indeed."

"They're either getting sloppy, or desperate, or both." James gave a wry smile. "That often happens when they start to feel the pressure of investigation. Rose spotted that the letter contained American spelling and terminology. The forger wrote about 'trucks' instead of 'lorries' and spelled 'favor' without a 'u.' That sort of thing."

"When criminals try to be creative." I shook my head. "And Mary Alice was tracking them. Look at the letter addressed to the War Department. She was even corresponding with officials in Washington about her suspicions."

James read the letter carefully, a line forming between his brows. "This suggests she was working with the authorities."

"Which gives us a whole different motive for her murder," I said quietly. "Someone killed her to stop her investigation."

James's eyes met mine. "Who?"

I took a deep breath. "Eleanor Crawford."

"This doesn't prove anything," James's tone had shifted.

"No, but this might." I pulled out the small photograph clipped from a newspaper that had been tucked inside Mary Alice's music folder. "Look at the note in the margin."

James turned it over, reading aloud: "Ella Winters, Sterling City, October 1917.' And below that, 'Watch her.'"

The photograph showed a clear image of Eleanor Crawford, standing with a group of Red Cross volunteers.

"The fraud in Sterling City happened about six months ago, right?" I said quietly. "During the time that this 'Ella Winters' lived there. And now here she is in Timber Coulee, using a different name."

James was silent for a long moment, his mind clearly working through the implications. "This is all circumstantial, Amanda. Suggestive, but not proof."

I lowered my voice. "Eleanor has been asking very specific questions about soldiers' families—especially those receiving benefits or who might be vulnerable. Questions about exactly the kind of information that would be needed to forge documents or send convincing fake letters."

"Like the one the Thorntons received about their son. And the one Rose MacTavish received about Callan."

"Yes. And James—I believe she did something to Mildred Abernathy. Mildred would never abandon her students or her life in Timber Coulee without a word. Something happened to her."

James straightened, his sheriff's demeanor fully in place now. "I need to send some more telegrams. If Eleanor Crawford, posing as Ella Winters, was involved in the Sterling City—"

"There's no time," I interrupted. "The choir is meeting tonight for the final rehearsal before tomorrow's concert. Eleanor will be there. And if she suspects we're onto her—"

"She might run." James's expression was grim. "Or worse."

Our eyes met, and in that moment, the tension of the past days dissolved. He believed me. More important, he understood what was at stake.

"What do you need me to do?" I asked.

"Nothing." His tone was firm. "This is sheriff business now. I'll handle it."

I straightened my spine. "James, this is my shop. My choir. My niece who was under suspicion. I'm involved whether you like it or not."

He studied me for a long moment, then nodded with noticeable reluctance. "All right. But you follow my lead. No heroics."

I almost giggled at the absurdity of the warning. "I promise not to tackle any suspected criminals."

A ghost of a smile touched his lips. "I remember what you did to Lucas Baker a while back."

"That was different. He deserved it."

"And Eleanor Crawford doesn't?"

"Oh, she deserves worse, if my suspicions are true. But I'll leave that to the justice system. After we catch her."

James checked his pocket watch. "Rehearsal starts at seven?"

"Yes, at the town hall. Molly's already there, helping Judith set up."

"We should get going, then." He gathered the evidence.

Outside, the evening had deepened, streetlamps casting pools of golden light on the wet sidewalks. As we walked side by side toward the town hall, I felt James's hand brush mine, briefly, deliberately.

"Whatever happens tonight," he said quietly, "just know that I never truly believed Molly could have done this."

I glanced at him, finding his eyes warm in the lamplight. "Then why did you let me think you did?"

"Because I can't let my personal feelings get in the way of an investigation. I needed clear evidence. And I needed you to fight for her," he said simply. "I needed you to care enough to find the truth. I knew you wouldn't stop until you did."

I understood then. It hadn't been about Molly at all. It had been about me—about pulling me out of the fog of grief and fear that had enveloped me since finding Mary Alice's body. About giving me purpose, direction.

"You're a devious man, Sheriff Holcomb." But there was no heat in my words.

"Only when necessary, Miss Parrish."

For the first time in days, my heart lightened.

Chapter Twenty-Five

The town hall windows glowed, lit from within against the gathering twilight. From inside came the harmonizing of voices—the choir warming up for the final rehearsal before the mayor's patriotic festival. James and I paused at the entrance.

"I've sent word to Peterson to be ready with backup," James murmured. "But we need to be cautious. If she's as dangerous as we suspect, we don't want to spook her."

Anxiety churned in my stomach. "How do you want to handle this?"

"Let me observe first. I'll sit in the back. You join the rehearsal like normal."

"And then?"

"And then we wait for the right moment." He touched my elbow gently. "Do be circumspect, Amanda. Don't let on that you suspect anything."

We entered separately—James slipping quietly into a back row of chairs while I made my way to the choir stands where the altos were gathered. Molly, seated with the sopranos, caught my eye and raised a questioning eyebrow. I gave her a barely perceptible shake of my head, warning her to act naturally.

Eleanor sat at the piano, her fingers dancing across the keys as she led the choir through "The Star-Spangled Banner." Her face was animated, Southern charm on full display as she called out encouragement.

"That's it, ladies! Y'all are soundin' just heavenly! Now remember, tomorrow this hall will be filled with proud patriots, so let's give this next part all the spirit it deserves!"

Judith smiled in approval and kept time with her baton as the choir launched into the next section with renewed vigor. I joined in, watching Eleanor from the corner of my eye. Nothing in her demeanor suggested she was a fraud or a murderer. She was the picture of enthusiastic dedication.

The rehearsal continued, with Judith offering occasional suggestions for improvement. I found it hard to concentrate, my attention split between the music and watching for any signal from James. While we took a short recess, he spoke quietly with Deputy Peterson, who had arrived and positioned himself just outside the side door, out of Eleanor's line of sight.

"Amanda, sugar!" Eleanor waved me over to the piano during a pause between songs. "I was hopin' you might help me with somethin'."

My heartbeat thundered as I approached, forcing a smile. "Of course. What is it?"

"This passage is just givin' me fits." She pointed to the sheet music for "America the Beautiful." "Could you take a look at measure twenty-seven? Somethin' doesn't sound quite right."

I leaned over the music, acutely aware of how close she was—this woman who had likely strangled Mary Alice with knitting yarn and arranged those needles on her chest. Her perfume was subtle, her hands perfectly manicured as they rested on the piano keys.

"It looks correct to me." I fought to keep my voice steady. "Perhaps the altos are coming in too strongly."

"You might be right." She smiled up at me, dark eyes crinkling. "By the way, has Molly received any news from Clarence recently?"

The question seemed innocent enough, but something in her tone made the hair on the back of my neck rise. Was she fishing for information?

"Not that I'm aware of. You'd have to ask Molly."

"It's so important to keep those connections with our boys overseas, isn't it? Letters, packages . . . sometimes it's all they have to keep their spirits up." Her fingers absently played a melancholy chord. "I'm certain he appreciates every little thing she sends to him, over there in Alsace-Lorraine."

My breath caught. I'd never mentioned Clarence was in Alsace-Lorraine. In fact, I hadn't even known his exact location. His letters came heavily censored, omitting such details. I only had a vague idea that he was somewhere in Europe. Ice water coursed through my veins as I realized she had been gathering information about Molly just as she had with other families.

"Indeed, he does." I struggled to maintain my composure. Over Eleanor's shoulder, I could see James moving slowly closer, his attention locked on our conversation.

"Ladies!" Judith called with a whack of her baton. "Let's take it from the top once more, then we'll call it a night."

As everyone returned to their positions, I caught a flash of movement at the hall entrance—Deputy Miller arriving with another officer. They hid themselves just outside the doors. James gave me a slight nod. They were ready.

We began singing "America the Beautiful," Eleanor's accompaniment flawless as always. I scanned the room. All exits were now covered by James's deputies. Whatever was about to happen, there would be no escape for Eleanor.

As the song reached its final verse, the hall doors opened again. A woman stepped inside—thin, pale, with auburn hair partially hidden under a modest hat. She moved quietly toward the back row of chairs, but not before I recognized her.

Mildred Abernathy.

Eleanor's fingers faltered on the keys as she spotted Mildred. For just a moment, her cheerful mask slipped, revealing something cold and calculating beneath. Then she recovered, finishing the song with professional precision.

"Ladies, that was just beautiful!" she exclaimed as the final notes faded. "Y'all have worked so hard, and it shows!"

Judith grinned. "I think we're ready for tomorrow. Thank you all for your dedication during such a difficult time."

As the choir members gathered their things, James moved forward, positioning himself strategically between Eleanor and the nearest exit. I held my breath, watching the scene unfold as if in slow motion.

"Mrs. Crawford." James's voice carried across the now-quieting room. "Or should I say, Miss Winters?"

Eleanor looked up, her expression a perfect blend of confusion and innocence. "I beg your pardon, Sheriff? I'm afraid I don't understand."

"I think you do." James approached the piano, his manner calm but authoritative. "Deputy Peterson has just informed me that we've received some interesting telegrams from Sterling City. About a woman named Ella Winters who was involved in defrauding war widows and soldiers' families."

A ripple of confused murmurs ran through the remaining choir members. Eleanor laughed, the sound brittle and forced.

"Well, that's just ridiculous! I don't know any Ella Winters. There must be some mistake."

Mildred Abernathy stepped forward from the shadows. "There's no mistake." Her voice was quiet but firm. "I thought your face rang a bell from the moment you arrived in Timber Coulee. You were calling yourself Nora Campbell when you worked at the Ladies' Aid Society in Portland last year, weren't you? My sister Peggy was involved in that organization, and there were some irregularities with the accounts."

P is for Peggy, I thought, remembering the scrap of a letter I'd found in Mildred's cottage. Peggy in Portland, who'd sent Mildred a letter warning her to be careful, as any good sister would.

Eleanor's face hardened, the Southern belle persona evaporating. "Mildred," she said coldly. "I thought we had an understandin'."

"You threatened my family." Mildred's voice shook. "You said if I didn't stop helping Mary Alice, you'd make sure my nephew was reported as a draft dodger."

"Hold on," James said. "Perhaps I am mistaken. Perhaps Ella Winters isn't the correct name. I must be thinking of Nora Campbell. No, wait, Nora Campbell was in Portland." I could tell James was enjoying this. "Could it be . . . Nell Delaney?"

Gasps echoed through the hall as the choir members realized what was happening. Eleanor's eyes darted around the room, assessing her options. I could almost see her calculating the odds of escape, noting the deputies at each exit.

"Sheriff, I don't know what tales this woman has been spinnin', but I assure you—"

"Save it," James interrupted. "We have evidence linking you to fraudulent operations in three different cities under three different identities. And we have reason to believe you killed Mary Alice Wellington to prevent her from exposing your scheme here in Timber Coulee."

Eleanor's expression changed again, hardening into something cruel. "You can't prove that."

"Perhaps not yet," James agreed. "But Mrs. Abernathy witnessed you arguing with Mary Alice the night she died. And we have this." He held up the newspaper photograph we'd found in Mary Alice's folder.

For a moment, no one moved. Then, with unexpected speed, Eleanor lunged for her handbag on top of the piano. James was faster, seizing her wrist before she could reach whatever was inside.

"Nell Delaney," he said formally, "you're under arrest for fraud and suspected homicide."

As Deputy Peterson moved to handcuff her, Eleanor's composure cracked entirely. "You don't understand," she hissed. "Those benefits were going to waste! Those families didn't deserve them—they weren't really suffering! I put that money to better use!"

"By stealing from war widows and frightening families like the Thorntons and the Fairmonts?" I interjected.

"It wasn't just me," she spat, her accent completely gone now. "I had help—you think I could manage all those documents alone?"

At that moment, the hall door swung open again. Deputy Miller entered, firmly gripping the arm of a familiar man—William Crawford, Eleanor's brother-in-law.

Except that wasn't right.

"We found him at the train station, Sheriff," Deputy Miller announced. "Ticket to Chicago in his pocket, along with these." He held up a leather case and lifted the lid. It appeared to contain various papers and stamps.

James's jaw tightened. "William Crawford. Or should I say, Walter Delaney?"

The man's face remained impassive, though I detected a slight twitch at the corner of his mouth.

"Walter?" I gasped, looking between Eleanor and the man. "But I thought—"

"A clever deception," James explained, his eyes never leaving Walter. "This man is Walter Delaney, Nell Delaney's brother—not her brother-in-law. There is no William Crawford nor Walter Crawford—at least not one relevant to this case. No record of a Walter Crawford serving with the military in France, either."

A dim memory fluttered in my mind of the way Eleanor had stuttered over his name that day at the hotel—'W-w-William'—perhaps she'd nearly said 'Walter' by mistake.

A collective gasp went up from the choir as all eyes turned toward the pair. Walter Delaney's dignified demeanor finally cracked as his gaze locked with Eleanor's.

"You told me you'd handled her," he said coldly to Eleanor, nodding toward Mildred. "You said there wouldn't be any witnesses."

"Walter, be quiet," Eleanor hissed, but it was too late.

"Mr. Delaney," James continued, "you're under arrest for conspiracy to commit fraud, forgery, and accessory to murder."

"Murder?" For the first time, Walter looked genuinely shocked. "I had nothing to do with that. That was all Nell. I create documents, forge signatures—I don't kill people."

Eleanor's face contorted with rage. "You coward! After everything I've done to make this work!"

As the deputies led the pair away, the hall erupted in shocked conversations. I made my way to a pale and shaken Mildred.

"Welcome home. Are you all right?" I took her hands in mine.

She nodded. "I've been staying with my sister in Portland. When I got word from Sheriff Holcomb that it was safe to return, I came as quickly as I could."

"Eleanor forced you to leave town?"

"She knew I was helping Mary Alice discover discrepancies in the Ladies' Aid financial records—donations for the war effort that never reached their destination." Mildred shuddered. "She threatened my family. I was too frightened to tell anyone."

James joined us, his expression grave but satisfied. "Mrs. Abernathy, your testimony will be invaluable in building our case."

"What about Mary Alice?" I asked. "What do you remember about that night?"

"Mary Alice telephoned me that afternoon," Mildred's voice trembled at the memory. "She was distraught—said she'd been a fool. Eleanor had convinced her to share confidential information from the Ladies' Aid files, supposedly to help military families. But when funds started disappearing and strange letters arrived, Mary Alice realized she'd been manipulated. She felt responsible for every family that had been targeted."

"So that's why she investigated on her own." Pieces were falling into place. "She was trying to make amends."

Mildred's face clouded. "She couldn't bear to admit publicly how she'd been duped. Her pride wouldn't allow it. She was determined to expose the scheme herself, to make things right. She said she'd written to the War Department about the fraud scheme and made carbon copies. She was bringing them to rehearsal to show me—said she didn't feel safe keeping them at home. She and I stayed late to review the evidence she'd gathered."

"That's when you two asked for permission to stay late to practice Mary Alice's solo," I said.

Mildred nodded. "We thought everyone had gone. But as Mary Alice was showing me her documentation about the missing funds, Eleanor appeared from somewhere. She must have been hiding there all during rehearsal, waiting for everyone to leave."

"So Moxie hadn't detected mice in the wall that evening, after all," I muttered, more to myself than to anyone else "Just one big rat, hiding behind the cello display." I remembered the sudden sneeze I'd heard as I left the shop that night. Most likely it had come from Eleanor, in reaction to Moxie. All at once, I recalled Moxie's peculiar behavior around Eleanor. "He knew," I whispered. Moxie had alerted to her scent that night as she lurked in the shop—waiting for Mary Alice. *If only I'd*—but, no. The time for speculating what I should or should not have done was over. Time to move on.

Mildred was still speaking. "Mary Alice confronted her immediately, said she had proof of fraud. Eleanor became . . . frightening. So cold, nothing like the charming woman we'd known. She demanded the documents. I—I panicked and ran. Mary Alice told me to go, said she could handle Eleanor herself."

As the truth about Mary Alice's last moments emerged, tears trickled down Mildred's cheeks. "If I'd just stayed with her, maybe I could have helped her. Maybe she'd still be alive."

James shook his head. "You were being threatened, Mrs. Abernathy. You did what you had to do."

"I know I should have sent word to you right away," Mildred admitted. "But Eleanor threatened my family. Said she had people watching them, that they'd suffer if I spoke to anyone, that she knew people in power, and she'd report on my nephew for draft-dodging—all false, of course. I was terrified. I packed what I could, but the last train had already departed for the night. I had to wait until morning, every moment fearing she would come for me next. When I finally boarded that train, I was looking over my shoulder the entire time. I never even got a good look at what Mary Alice wanted to show me."

"She was corresponding with military officials," James explained. "Apparently, she'd heard of such fraud schemes before and recognized the signs here."

"The carbon copies were in Mary Alice's music folder all along," I added. "Hidden in the back, behind 'America the Beautiful,' along with all of her notes on the situation. Most likely that's what she intended to show you. We found them when a leak caused us to dry out all the choir music."

Mildred looked stricken. "So she was right. All her questions about military payments, all her seemingly critical comments—"

"Were part of her investigation," James finished. "She was trying to identify vulnerable families and protect them."

"And the Delaneys? How did their scheme work, exactly?" The full scope of their deception strained belief.

James's face darkened. "From what we've gathered, Nell would position herself as a lone woman in communities with military connections—churches, women's groups, aid societies. She'd cultivate relationships, gain trust, and collect information on families with soldiers overseas."

"Meanwhile, in a different city, Walter would use that information to send official-looking letters demanding payments for fictional 'insurance premiums' or 'allotment adjustments,'" I added. "The letters threatened jail or other punishments if families didn't comply."

"And people paid?" Mildred asked, appalled.

"Many did," James confirmed. "The letters looked authentic—Walter has experience as a clerk in a government office. He knew how to make documents appear official. And the amounts were calculated to be just burdensome enough to hurt, but not so large that most families couldn't manage."

"What a horrible way to prey on people's fears during wartime." Disgust rose within my throat.

"They've been operating for at least two years, starting even before the U. S. entered the war," James continued. "Moving from town to town across three states. The authorities believe they've stolen thousands of dollars."

The irony wasn't lost on me. Mary Alice Wellington, with her sharp tongue and abrasive manner, had been working to protect the very people she seemed to criticize—and to atone for her own mistake in trusting Eleanor.

"It all makes sense now," Mildred said quietly. "Mary Alice told me how Eleanor first approached her, praising her organizational skills and appealing to her compassion for the soldiers' families. Mary Alice gave her access to the Ladies' Aid records, believing she was helping. When she realized what was happening, she was too ashamed to come forward immediately. She felt she needed to solve it herself. But it proved too overwhelming—eventually she had to enlist my help in deciphering some of the details. I guess she trusted me because I'm good with figures. And because I'm family. *Was* family."

I slid an arm around her slumping shoulders. "Her questions about military service weren't unpatriotic at all," I mused. "They were her awkward attempts to identify which families might be vulnerable to the Delaneys' scheme—and to protect them, in her own Mary Alice way."

Judith approached. "Mildred, we've all been so worried. May I drive you home?"

"Yes, I'd appreciate that." Arms linked, they walked together toward the exit.

As the hall gradually emptied, I found myself standing with James near the piano where, minutes earlier, Eleanor had sat playing patriotic songs as if she were the most loyal citizen in town.

"How did you know?" James asked quietly. "What first made you suspect her?"

I smiled ruefully. "Moxie."

"Your cat?"

"Believe it or not, he took an instant dislike to her, and he usually likes everybody. The last time he reacted so badly, the stranger turned out to be that charlatan, Lucas Baker. And then there was her accent."

"What about her accent?"

"It was inconsistent," I explained. "Usually, it was thick as molasses. But when I overheard her talking to

William—I mean, Walter—at the hotel, it was barely noticeable. And she got careless—claimed to write for a magazine that doesn't even exist. I'm sure she never anticipated we'd find out. I don't know how she dug up the information, other than getting innocent people to confide in her, but she seemed to know too many details about too many people too quickly, like she had an inside source or was simply probing too deeply into people's affairs."

Admiration shone in James's eyes. "You'd make a good detective, Amanda Parrish."

"I prefer music shop owner," I replied. "Less exciting, but also less likely to involve murderers."

His hand found mine in the dimming light of the hall. "I'm sorry I let you believe Molly was a suspect."

"You were doing your job," I conceded. "And it worked out in the end."

"It did." His fingers tightened around mine. "Though I'd prefer not to go through something like that in the future."

The way he said "future"—as if ours might be intertwined in some way—made my heart flutter in a most unprofessional manner.

"The concert is still on for tomorrow." I hastened to change the subject before my feelings became embarrassingly obvious. "Will you be attending, Sheriff?"

"I wouldn't miss it." His eyes never left mine. "After all, I hear the alto section is particularly fine this year."

For the first time in weeks, I laughed freely. Tomorrow would bring paperwork, statements, and the beginnings of a complex legal case. But tonight, walking home with James beside me under a sky full of stars, I felt only relief—and the tentative stirrings of something that felt remarkably like joy.

Chapter Twenty-Six

The town hall was filled to capacity for the patriotic concert. Red, white, and blue bunting festooned the walls, interspersed with posters of a beckoning Uncle Sam and pleas to buy Liberty Bonds. Small American flags had been distributed to each audience member. The mood was jubilant, not just for the celebration of our country, but for the restoration of peace to our small town.

News of the Delaneys' arrests had spread through Timber Coulee like wildfire. By morning, everyone knew that the charming Southern pianist and her supposed brother-in-law were actually Nell and Walter Delaney, a brother-and-sister team who had been running an elaborate scheme to defraud soldiers' families, and that Mary Alice Wellington had died trying to expose them.

The narrative had shifted overnight. Mary Alice, once considered the choir's most difficult member, was now spoken of with reverent tones as a hero who had given her life protecting our community. Mildred Abernathy had been welcomed back with open arms, her place at the piano restored. And Molly—my dear Molly—had been completely exonerated, the whispers and sidelong glances replaced with apologetic smiles.

As we assembled behind the curtain, waiting for our cue to take the stage, I scanned the crowd through a small opening. James sat in the third row, looking handsome in his freshly pressed uniform. Next to him was an empty seat—saved for me after the choir's portion of the program.

"Ladies." Judith gathered us in a circle. "This performance is dedicated to Mary Alice Wellington, whose courage and sacrifice we now understand. Let us sing tonight in her honor, and for all those who have given of themselves for our great nation."

Heads nodded solemnly. Even Beatrice Fairmont, who had so often clashed with Mary Alice, wiped away a tear.

The curtain rose to enthusiastic applause. Mildred struck the opening chords to "The Star-Spangled Banner" and everyone rose to their feet. As we sang, a profound sense of gratitude—for this music that bound us together, for this town that had become my home, for the friends and family who had stood by me through this ordeal, and above all, for the God who loved and protected us all—settled over me.

After the final chord came to an end, Mayor Blackwood stepped forward to address the audience.

"Ladies and gentlemen," his voice carried strongly across the hall, "we gather tonight not only to remember those who gave their lives for our country, but also to honor the resilience of our community. The past weeks have tested us sorely, but Timber Coulee has emerged stronger and more united."

Murmurs of agreement rippled through the crowd.

Mayor Blackwood's expression grew more serious. "I've received word this afternoon from our newspaper correspondent in Boise—sketchy details, mind you, but it appears our American boys are finally in it, somewhere near a French town called Cantigny. The reports suggest this is more than just a skirmish." He paused, letting the weight of his words settle over the audience. "We don't know the particulars yet, but we do know our brave soldiers are writing history as we speak."

A hush fell over the hall. Beatrice Fairmont's hand flew to her throat, no doubt thinking of Henry. Molly and I exchanged worried glances, our thoughts with Clarence. In the audience, other mothers, fathers, wives, and daughters shifted uneasily in their seats. The reality of war—distant for so long—suddenly felt immediate and pressing.

"Which makes tonight's gathering all the more meaningful." The mayor's voice gained strength. "Thanks to the diligent work of our sheriff and his deputies,"—he gestured toward James, who acknowledged the recognition with a modest nod—"dangerous criminals have been removed from our midst. Justice will be served for Mary Alice Wellington, and the funds stolen from our soldiers' families will be restored."

This brought increased applause, particularly from the Thornton family, who were seated near the front. Mr. Thornton had his arm protectively around Viola, who had been deemed a victim of manipulation rather than a willing accomplice. She would face no charges, though the shame of her involvement would take longer to fade.

"The Crawford-Delaney case has revealed how vulnerable we can be during these troubled times," the mayor continued. "Walter Delaney used his knowledge of government procedures to create convincing forgeries, while his sister Nell used her charm to gather sensitive information from unsuspecting families. Posing as a war widow gave Nell instant credibility and sympathy in communities supporting the war effort. No one questions a grieving widow's interest in soldiers' families, and it gave Walter freedom to operate separately as her 'brother-in-law' without raising suspicions. Together, they preyed upon the fears and patriotism of our citizens."

He paused, his expression solemn. "Let tonight's concert remind us of what truly matters—faith, community, and the unwavering American spirit that sustains us through the darkest hours."

More applause followed when he introduced the next song. As we sang our way through the patriotic program, I caught Molly's eye during "My Country 'Tis of Thee." She grinned at me, looking truly carefree for the first time since Mary Alice's death.

As I sang the familiar lyrics, my gaze found James in the audience, his eyes never leaving mine. The words about freedom took on new meaning. I felt free not just as an American, but as a woman no longer constrained by grief or guilt.

After the concert concluded to enthusiastic applause, I joined James in the audience for the mayor's closing remarks.

"Timber Coulee has always been a town of good people," Mayor Blackwood declared. "People who look out for each other, who stand together in times of trouble. This unfortunate incident has only proven what we already knew—that the strength of our community cannot be broken, not by fraud, not by murder, not even by war."

He raised his hand. "I propose three cheers for our Rocky Mountain Meadowlarks, who refused to be silenced even in their darkest hour!"

The audience rose, cheering loudly. Judith looked close to tears as she acknowledged the ovation with a deep bow.

The crowd began to disperse, and James leaned closer to me.

"The War Department sent a telegram this afternoon," he said quietly. "They've begun notifying all the families who were defrauded by the Delaneys."

"How many?" I asked.

"At least thirty so far, across three states. The investigators found Walter's ledger at their lodgings—detailed records of every penny they stole. Apparently, he was quite proud of his bookkeeping skills, though not wise enough to destroy the evidence."

"What will happen to them?"

"Walter has already started talking, trying to save himself by providing evidence against Nell. Claims he was just the paperwork man, that she was the mastermind and the one who killed Mary Alice." James shook his head in disgust. "No honor among thieves—or murderers."

"Do you believe him? About not being involved in the murder?"

"It's possible," James admitted. "But he profited from their scheme and helped create the circumstances that led to Mary Alice's death. He'll serve time either way."

The hall emptying around us, James turned to me, his eyes warm in the lamplight.

"That was beautiful," he said softly.

"The concert?"

"Your singing." His hand found mine, hidden between the folds of my skirt. "I'd forgotten how lovely your voice is. Sarah always said you were the best alto in the choir."

The mention of Sarah's name no longer brought pain—just a gentle recognition of what had been, and what might now be.

"James," I began, but he shook his head.

"Let me say this, Amanda. I've spent three years hiding behind my grief, using it as an excuse to keep people at a distance. To keep *you* at a distance." His fingers tightened around mine. "That ends tonight."

My heart stuttered, then galloped. "What are you saying?"

"I'm saying that life is too short and too precious to waste. Mary Alice taught us that. She could be difficult, even unpleasant at times, but she died trying to protect others." He took a deep breath. "I don't want to look back years from now and regret the chances I didn't take."

Around us, the few townspeople who remained congratulated choir members, discussed the revelations of the past days, and made plans for tomorrow. But in that moment, there was only James and me, and the possibility stretching before us like an unwritten melody.

"I believe Sarah would approve," I murmured.

"I know she would." His smile held a hint of remembered sadness, but mostly hope. "She always said we were two of a kind—stubborn as mules but worth the trouble."

I laughed, the sound surprising me with its freedom. "Did she really say that?"

"Often." He stood, offering me his arm. "May I walk you home, Miss Parrish?"

"I'd like that very much, Sheriff Holcomb."

As we made our way through the remnants of the crowd, I caught sight of Molly standing with Mildred and Judith. She noticed us, her eyes widening at our linked arms, then gave me a delighted smile and an exaggerated wink.

Outside, the spring night was warm and clear, stars scattered across the velvet sky like notes on a musical staff. The town square was quiet now, most residents having returned to their homes, secure in the knowledge that the danger had passed.

We paused in front of my house. The cottage was dark, but Moxie's orange face was illuminated by moonlight as he waited for my return in the window.

"I should go in." I made no move to release James's arm.

"You should." He remained equally motionless.

A moment stretched between us, full of unspoken possibilities. Then, with surprising gentleness, James leaned forward and pressed his lips to mine. It was a brief kiss, tender and somewhat tentative, but it carried the promise of more to come.

When he pulled away, his eyes searched mine. "I've wanted to do that for a very long time."

"I've wanted you to," I admitted. "For just as long."

He touched my cheek, a gesture so tender it nearly brought tears to my eyes. "Good night, Amanda. I'll see you tomorrow."

"Tomorrow." The word no longer held dread or fear, but lovely anticipation.

As I let myself into the house, Moxie greeted me with an affectionate headbutt against my ankles. I scooped him up, burying my face in his warm fur.

"We did it, Moxie," I whispered. "We found the truth."

He purred in response, as if to say he'd never doubted we would.

I smiled, thinking of James, of the music shop, of our place in this small town that had weathered a storm and emerged intact. My heart overflowed with thankfulness—for Molly's safety, for the truth revealed, and perhaps most surprisingly, for the promise of tomorrow with James.

"Now," I murmured, more to myself than to Moxie, "we move forward. We make music. We live."

And for the first time in a very long while, those simple things seemed like more than enough.

THE END

Author's Note

While the specific characters and events in *Something Wicked This Way Hums* are fictional, they are grounded in the genuine experiences, challenges, and vulnerabilities of American communities during the First World War. Although the US officially entered the war in April 1917 (despite President Woodrow Wilson's campaign promise to the contrary), some Americans did serve in Europe prior to that time through the American Expeditionary Forces (AEF).

Our story takes place in May 1918, during the final year of the war, when American forces were heavily engaged in France and the home front was fully mobilized for the war effort. The decisive Battle of Cantigny (May 28-31, 1918) was the first major American offensive of WWI, and news in that era would have traveled slowly to small towns, arriving as rumors and incomplete reports rather than detailed accounts.

Small-town America during World War I was characterized by intense patriotic fervor and community pressure to demonstrate loyalty through visible support of the war effort. This atmosphere of heightened emotion and suspicion created opportunities for manipulation by those with criminal intent. Fraudulent schemes targeting soldiers' families were unfortunately all too real. During and after World War I, criminals exploited the fears and patriotism of military families, preying on their natural concern for their loved ones and their unfamiliarity with military bureaucracy. The War Department eventually had to issue warnings about such fraud.

The home front activities portrayed—knitting socks for soldiers, Liberty Bond drives, Red Cross volunteering, and food conservation programs like "Wheatless Mondays" and "Meatless Tuesdays"—were genuine aspects of American civilian war support. Women's organizations, churches, and other community groups played crucial roles in supporting troops and their families, making them natural targets for the kind of infiltration and exploitation depicted in the story.

The 91st Infantry Division (nicknamed the "Wild West Division") served with distinction in France. The censorship of soldiers' mail and the various non-combat roles (like ambulance drivers and field medics) that were sometimes unfairly devalued by civilians all reflect historical realities.

The men and women who served overseas and those who supported them at home deserve to be remembered not only for their sacrifices, but also for their resilience in the face of those who would exploit their dedication to duty and country.

In Gratitude

To God be the glory.

I offer my deepest thanks to:

Pegg Thomas, wizard of wordsmithing;

Anita Aurit, Terese Luikens, and Grace Robinson, partners in writing, marketing, and mischief;

Linda Nelson, first reader and head cheerleader;

The women of the Thursday night Bible study at Kootenai Community Church;

and especially Thomas Leo, the very best husband a lady could wish for. You are my sunshine!

And thanks to you, dear reader, for taking a chance on my book. If you enjoyed the story, I'd be pleased as punch if you'd leave a review on Goodreads or Amazon or wherever you get your books. Please visit JenniferLamontLeo.com to sign up for my Reader Community, or drop me a line. I'd love to hear from you!

Also by the author

The Corrigan Sisters Series

You're the Cream in My Coffee

Ain't Misbehavin'

Wrap Your Troubles in Dreams

The Windy City Hearts Series

Moondrop Miracle

The Rose Keeper

Love's Grand Sweet Song

The Music Shop Mysteries Series

Murder on a High Note

Something Wicked This Way Hums

Snake in the Brass (*coming Fall 2025*)

Sneak Peek

Book Three in the Music Shop Mysteries Series

Coming up next in the Music Shop Mysteries series . . .

SNAKE IN THE BRASS

Toes are tapping and fingers snapping when a touring jazz band rolls up in Timber Coulee. But not everyone is happy about having such a brassy bunch of "outsiders" stirring things up, leading to murder, mayhem, and all that jazz. Will Amanda be able to restore harmony? Or will her amateur sleuthing strike a sour note with the local sheriff?

What's the Buzz?

Reviews are pure gold to an author! If you enjoyed this book and want to help spread the word, post reviews on book-oriented websites like Goodreads, Amazon, and BookBub. Reviews can be short or as long as you like. And please talk about the book, in person and on social media. Word-of-mouth is still the best way to promote just about anything!

Let's stay in touch. Please stop by and say hello.

Visit JenniferLamontLeo.com (Join my Reader Community for book news, exclusive content, and more), or look for me on Facebook and other social media.

Listen to my podcast, A Sparkling Vintage Life! (Listen online at sparklingvintagelife.com or subscribe in your favorite podcast app)

www.ingramcontent.com/pod-product-compliance
Lightning Source LLC
Chambersburg PA
CBHW032357310726
48973CB00007B/2046